# PAN

# KNUT HAMSUN

# PAN

*From Lieutenant Thomas Glahn's papers*

*Translated from the Norwegian by*
JAMES W. McFARLANE

THE NOONDAY PRESS
A DIVISION OF FARRAR, STRAUS
AND GIROUX
NEW YORK

Copyright 1956 by The Noonday Press, Inc.
*Library of Congress Catalog Card Number: 56-12295*

SBN 374.5.0016.9

*First Noonday Paperbound Edition, 1956*

*Thirteenth printing, 1970*

MANUFACTURED IN THE UNITED STATES OF AMERICA
by The Murray Printing Company

*This Edition is dedicated to*
Johan Nilsen Nagel

# I

THESE last few days I have thought and thought of the Nordland summer's endless day. I sit here and think of it, and of a hut I lived in, and of the forest behind the hut; and I have taken to writing about it, just for my own amusement and to while away the time. Time drags; it does not pass as quickly as I should like, although I have no cares and lead the gayest of lives. I am perfectly content with everything, and thirty is no great age. A few days ago I received a couple of bird's feathers from far away, from one who need not have sent them; just two green feathers folded in a sheet of paper with a coronet on it and fastened with a seal. It amused me to see two so fiendishly green feathers. Otherwise there is nothing to trouble me except a touch of arthritis now and then in my left foot, the result of an old shot wound that healed up long ago.

I remember that time went much faster two years ago, incomparably faster than now; the summer was gone before I realised it. It was two years ago, in 1855—I want to write about it to amuse myself—that something happened to me: or else I dreamt it. By now I have forgotten many things that happened then, for I have scarcely given them a thought since. But I remember that the nights were very light. Many things struck me as odd: the year still had its twelve months, but night turned into day and there was never a star to be seen in the sky. And the people I met were strange, and of a different nature from the people I had known before. Sometimes a single night was enough to make them blossom from childhood into all their splendour, mature and fully grown. There was no magic in this, but I had never known the like of it before. No, never.

In a big, white-washed house down by the sea I met someone who for a short while filled my thoughts. She is no longer always in my memory, not now—no, I have quite forgotten her. But I do recall all the other things, the cries of the sea birds, the hunting in the forest, my nights, and all the warm hours of summer. It was in any case by sheer chance that I met her; and had it not been for that chance she would never have lain in my thoughts for a single day.

From my hut I could see a confusion of islands and rocks and skerries, a little of the sea, a few blue-tinged peaks; and behind the hut lay the forest, an immense forest. I was filled with joy and thankfulness at the smell of the roots and leaves and the rich, fatty redolence of the firs, so like the smell of bone-marrow. Only in the forest did all within me find peace, my soul became tranquil and full of might. Day after day I went up into the hills, Aesop at my side; and I wished for no more than to be allowed to go there day after day, although the ground was still half covered with snow and soft ice. My only companion was Aesop; now I have Cora but then I had Aesop, my dog whom I later shot.

Often in the evening when I returned to the hut after a day's shooting, a warm sense of home-coming would run through my whole body; I trembled with inward pleasure and I would go and chat to Aesop about the good time we were having. ' Well, now we'll make a fire and roast ourselves a bird on the hearth,' I would say. ' What do you say to that? ' And when that was done and we had both eaten, Aesop would creep away to his place behind the hearth, while I would light a pipe and lie down for a while on my plank bed and listen to the muffled whisperings of the forest. There was a slight breeze, the wind bore straight upon the hut and I could hear the calling of the grouse far away in the hills behind. Apart from that, all was quiet.

And many a time I fell asleep where I lay, fully dressed just as I was, and did not wake until the sea birds began their screeching. Then, when I looked out of the window, I could catch a glimpse of the large white buildings down at the trading station, the landing stage of Sirilund, the store where I bought my bread; and I remained lying there a while, full of wonder that I should find myself here in a hut in Nordland on the edge of a forest.

Then, over beside the hearth, Aesop would shake his long lean body, rattling his collar and yawning and wagging his tail; and I would jump up after these three or four hours sleep, refreshed and filled with gladness towards all things, all things.

So passed many a night.

## 2

IT can rain and it can blow—these are not the things that count; often on a rainy day a small joy possesses one so that one retires into a private happiness. One stands looking straight ahead, laughing softly now and then and glancing around. What is one thinking of? A clear pane in a window, a ray of sunlight on the pane, a view across to a little stream and perhaps to a break of blue in the sky. It need not be more.

At other times even unusual events cannot jolt a man out of a dreary and cheerless mood; in the middle of a ballroom he can sit unmoved, indifferent, and impassive. For it is within ourselves that the sources of joy and sorrow lie.

I remember one particular day. I had gone down

to the coast. I was caught in the rain and I went into a boathouse that was standing open and sat for a while. I hummed a little to myself, but joylessly, just to pass the time. Aesop was with me and sat up to listen; I stop humming and listen as well; voices can be heard outside, someone is approaching. A chance event, and quite a natural one! A party of two men and a girl come stumbling in on me. They shout to each other, laughing: 'Quick! we can shelter in here a while.'

I rose.

One of the men was wearing a white shirt with unstarched front that was now sodden from the rain and baggy. In this wet shirt front was pinned a diamond clasp. On his feet he had long pointed shoes that looked somewhat foppish. I greeted the man; it was Herr Mack, the trader; I remembered him from the store where I had bought bread. He had even invited me to visit him at home sometime, but I had not been there yet.

'Ah, we meet again!' he said as he caught sight of me. 'We were on our way out to the mill, but had to turn back. What weather, eh? Now, when are you coming down to Sirilund, Lieutenant?' He introduced the little black-bearded man with him, a doctor, who was living near the annex church.

The girl lifted her veil a little from her face and began to talk to Aesop in a low voice. I noticed her jacket and could see from the lining and the button-holes that it had been dyed. Herr Mack introduced her also, she was his daughter, Edvarda.

Edvarda glanced at me through her veil and then went on whispering to the dog and read what was on his collar: 'So, you are called Aesop, are you? . . . Doctor, who was Aesop? All I remember is that he wrote fables. Wasn't he a Phrygian? ——No, I don't know.'

A mere child, a schoolgirl. I looked at her; she was tall but had no figure, about fifteen or sixteen, with long brown hands and no gloves. Perhaps she had looked up 'Aesop' in an encyclopedia that same afternoon.

Herr Mack questioned me about my shooting. What did I shoot most? I could use one of his boats whenever I liked, I had only to say. The Doctor did not speak a word. When the party went, I noticed that the Doctor limped slightly and used a stick.

I strolled home in the same vacant mood as before, humming apathetically. That meeting in the boathouse did not affect me one way or the other. What I remembered best from the whole affair was Herr Mack's soaking shirt front with the diamond clasp, which was wet too and not very brilliant.

# 3

THERE was a boulder outside my hut, a big grey boulder. It always seemed by its expression to be well-disposed towards me; it was as if it saw me as I came past and knew me again. I used to like making my way past this boulder when I went out in the mornings, and it was as though I left a good friend there who would be waiting when I got back.

And then up in the forest began the hunting. Perhaps I would shoot something, perhaps not . . .

Beyond the islands the sea lay heavy and becalmed. Many a time I stood and looked at it when I was high up in the hills; on still days the ships hardly moved at all and I could often see the same sail for three days, small and white like a gull on the water. But if the wind were to change, the mountains in the distance would almost disappear. The weather grew stormy, a south-west gale, a drama to which I was spectator. Everything was in a haze. Earth and sky merged, the sea tossed itself in the air in a fantastic dance, into the shapes of men and horses and tattered banners. I stood in the lee of an overhanging rock and thought of many things; my soul was tense. God

knows, I thought, what I am witnessing to-day
and why the sea opens before my very eyes!
Perhaps at this moment I gaze into the earth's
inner brain, see its workings, how it seethes!
Aesop was restless, now and then he put his nose
in the air and sniffed, weather-sick, his legs quivering nervously. As I said nothing to him, he lay
down between my feet and looked out to sea as I
did. And not a cry, not a human voice to be
heard anywhere, only the dull roar of the storm
about my head. Far out, there lay a reef, it lay
alone; when the sea dashed against its rocks, it
reared up like a demented twisting thing, or perhaps like a sea-god rising wet from the waves and
looking out over the world, snorting so that his
hair and beard stood out round his head like a
wheel. Then he plunged down again into the
raging surf.

And in the midst of the storm, a little coal-black
steamer put in from the sea. . . .

When I went down to the landing stage in the
afternoon, the little coal-black steamer had come
into the harbour; it was the mail boat. Lots of
people had gathered on the quayside to have a
look at the rare visitor; I noticed that they all
without exception had blue eyes, however different
they might be in other ways. A young girl with
a white woollen scarf stood a little apart; she had
very dark hair, and the white scarf showed up
sharply against it. She looked inquisitively at me,

at my leather clothes and my gun; when I spoke to her, she became embarrassed and turned her head away. I said: 'You should always wear that white scarf, it suits you.' Just then a burly man in an Icelander's jersey came up and joined her; he called her Eva. She was evidently his daughter. I knew the burly man, he was the smith, the local blacksmith. A few days ago he had put a new firing-pin in one of my guns. . . .

And rain and wind did their work and melted away the snow. For some days a chill atmosphere of unrest hung over the earth; rotten branches snapped and the crows collected in flocks and squawked. But it was not for long, the sun was near; one morning it rose up behind the forest. A sweet pang strikes through me when the sun comes; I throw my gun on my shoulder in silent rejoicing.

# 4

AT this time there was no lack of game; I shot what I wanted, a hare, a grouse, a ptarmigan, and when I happened to be down by the sea and within range of some sea bird or other, I shot that as well. They were good times, the days grew longer and the air clearer. I took enough for a couple of days and went off into the mountains;

I met Lapps who let me have cheese, small rich cheeses tasting of herbs. I went there more than once. On my way home again I always managed to shoot some sort of bird and put it in my bag. I sat down and put Aesop on the leash. Miles below me I could see the sea; the mountain sides were wet and black from the water running down them, dripping and rippling always to the same little melody. These little melodies far up in the mountains beguiled me for many an hour while I sat and looked around. Here is this little endless tune rippling on in solitude, I used to think, and nobody listens to it or thinks about it, but all the same it keeps rippling on to itself, keeps rippling on. And I no longer felt that the mountain was so wholly desolate when I could hear that rippling. Now and then something would happen: thunder would shake the earth, a lump of rock would break loose and plunge down to the sea, leaving behind it a trail of smoke and rubble; and at that Aesop would put his nose to the wind, puzzled, and sniff the smell of scorching he did not understand. When the melting snow cut deep rifts in the mountain-side, a shot or even a sharp cry was enough to dislodge large blocks and send them toppling down. . . .

An hour might pass, perhaps more, time went so swiftly. I unleashed Aesop, slung my bag over the other shoulder and set off for home. The day was ending. Down in the forest I hit unerringly

on my old familiar path, a narrow ribbon of a path
with the most curious twists and turns. I followed
every bend, taking my time; there was no hurry
and nobody was waiting for me at home. Free as
a king I went my way in the peace of the forest, as
leisurely as I pleased. All the birds were silent.
Only far away the grouse were calling; they were
always calling.

I came out of the wood and saw two people
ahead of me, two people wandering along; I over-
took them, one was Miss Edvarda, I recognised
her and greeted her; the Doctor was with her.
I had to show them my gun, they looked at my
compass and my bag; I invited them to my hut
and they promised to come some day.

Now it was evening. I went home, lit a fire,
roasted a bird and had a meal. To-morrow was
another day. . . .

It was quiet and hushed everywhere. I lay the
whole evening looking out of my window. An
enchanted light hung over field and forest at that
hour; the sun had set and coloured the horizon
with a fatty, red light, motionless like oil. Everywhere the sky was open and pure. I gazed into
the clear sea and it was as if I lay face to face with
the depths of the earth, and as if my beating heart
went out to those depths and was at home there.
God knows, I thought to myself, why the horizon
clothes itself in mauve and gold to-night; or perhaps there is some celebration above the world, a

celebration in grand style, with music from the stars and boat trips down the tides. It looks like that! And I closed my eyes and went along with the boat, and thought after thought sailed through my brain. . . .

So passed many a day.

I roamed about and noticed how the snow was turning to water and how the ice was breaking up. Many days I did not fire a shot when there was already food enough in the hut; I just ranged about in freedom, and I let time pass. Wherever I turned there was always just as much to see and hear; everything changed a little each day, and even the willow-scrub and the juniper stood and waited for the spring. I went out for instance to the mill which was still iced up; but the earth around it had been trodden through many and many a year, and bore witness that men had come with sacks of corn on their backs to have it ground. It was as though I walked there among men; and there were also many dates and letters carved on the walls.

Ah, well!

## 5

SHALL I write more? No, no. Only a little more to amuse myself; and because it whiles away the time to tell how spring came two years ago and how the land was looking. A slight fragrance rose from the earth and the sea; there was a sweet sulphurous smell from the old leaves rotting in the woods; and the magpies flew with twigs in their beaks and began building nests. A few days later the becks were swollen and began to foam, a butterfly or two appeared, and the fishermen returned from their fishing stations. The trader's two sloops came in heavy-laden with fish, and anchored off the drying grounds. Suddenly there was life and movement out on the biggest of the islands where the fish were to be dried on the rocks. I saw everything from my window.

But no noise reached the hut; I was alone and remained so. Now and then somebody would pass by; I saw Eva, the smith's daughter; she had got a few freckles on her nose.

' Where are you going? ' I asked her.

' To fetch firewood,' she answered quietly. She had a rope in her hand to carry the wood with, and she had her white scarf on her head. I watched her as she went, but she did not turn round.

Then many days went by before I saw anyone again.

Spring advanced and the forest grew lighter. It was a great delight to watch the thrushes sitting in the tree-tops, staring into the sun and screeching. Sometimes I was already up by two in the morning to share the joyous mood that radiated from bird and beast at sunrise.

Spring had come to me too, and my blood throbbed like the tramp of feet. I sat in the hut and thought of seeing to my fishing rods and hooks, but I did not move a finger to do anything about them; a glad, dark unease invaded my heart. Suddenly Aesop jumped up and stood there, his legs stiff, and gave a short yelp. Someone was coming to the hut; I snatched off my cap and heard Miss Edvarda's voice already at the door. She and the Doctor had come, kindly and unostentatiously, to visit me as they had promised.

'Yes, he is at home,' I heard her say. And she came forward, and gave me her hand just like a little girl. 'We were here yesterday as well, but you were not at home,' she explained.

She sat down on my plank bed, on the rug, and looked round the hut; the Doctor sat down beside me on the long bench. We talked together, chatted away happily; among other things I told them what animals there were in the forest, and what sorts of game I could no longer shoot because of the close season. At present it was the close season for grouse.

The Doctor did not have much to say this time either; but when his eye fell on my powder horn with the little figure of Pan on it, he began to explain the myth of Pan.

'But,' said Edvarda suddenly, 'what do you live on when it is close season for all game?'

'On fish,' I answered. 'Mostly on fish. There is always something to eat.'

'But of course you could come and eat with us,' she said. 'Last year there was an Englishman who had your hut, he used to come down and have a meal with us sometimes.'

Edvarda looked at me and I looked at her. In that instant I felt a stirring near my heart, like the flicker of a friendly greeting. It was the spring and the bright day——I have thought about it since. Moreover, I admired the curve of her eyebrows.

She said a few words about my hut. I had hung the walls with various skins and the wings of birds, and inside it was like a shaggy den. She approved of it. 'Yes, it is a den,' she said.

I had nothing really suitable to offer the visitors: I thought I might roast a bird, just for the fun of it; they could eat it in hunter's fashion, with their fingers. That might be amusing.

So I roasted the bird.

Edvarda told us about the Englishman. He was an eccentric old man, he talked aloud to himself. He was a Catholic, and wherever he went he had a little prayer-book, with red and black lettering, in his pocket.

'Perhaps he was an Irishman,' the Doctor suggested.

'An Irishman?'

'Yes, wouldn't he be, since he was a Catholic?'

Edvarda blushed; she stammered and looked away. 'Well, yes, perhaps he was an Irishman.'

From then on she lost her liveliness. I felt sorry for her and wanted to put things right again; I said: 'No, of course you are right in thinking that he was an Englishman; the Irish don't travel to Norway.'

We agreed to row out and have a look at the fish drying-grounds one day. . . .

When I had seen my guests a little on their way, I went back and set to work on my fishing tackle. My landing-net had been hanging over a nail near the door and the mesh had been damaged by rust in several places; I sharpened a few hooks, bent them on, and looked at the rest of the nets. How difficult it was to get anything done to-day! Irrelevant thoughts kept coming and going in my head; it occurred to me that it had been wrong to let Miss Edvarda remain sitting there the whole time on the plank bed instead of making room for her on the bench. Suddenly I saw before me her brown face and brown neck. She had tied her apron low on her hips to accentuate the length of her body, as was fashionable. Her thumb had a chaste and girlish look about it that touched me; and the few wrinkles on her knuckles were full of kindliness. She had a generous mouth, and her lips were red.

I stood up, opened the door and listened. I heard nothing, nor had I anything really to listen for. I shut the door again; Aesop got up from his place and saw that I was restless. It occurred to me that I might run after Miss Edvarda and ask her for some silk thread to repair my net with; it was not just a pretext, I could produce the net and show her the holes made in the mesh by the rust. I was already outside the door when I remembered that I had silk thread myself in my fly-book, more even than I needed. I went quietly back in, dispirited, since I already had some silk thread myself.

As I entered the hut, a breath of something strange met me; it was as though I were no longer alone there.

# 6

A MAN asked me whether I had stopped shooting; he had not once heard me firing up in the hills, although he had been out fishing in the bay for two days. No, I had not shot anything, I was staying at home in the hut until there was nothing left there to eat.

On the third day I did go out hunting. The forest was turning green, there was a smell of earth and of trees, the wild chive was already pushing up little green shoots through the frozen moss. I was lost in thought and sat down several times. I had not seen a soul for three days, except the fisherman I met yesterday. Perhaps I shall run into somebody this evening as I am going home, I thought, perhaps at the edge of the forest where I met the Doctor and Miss Edvarda the last time. They might well have gone there for a walk again, perhaps and perhaps not. But why did I think particularly of those two? I shot a couple of ptarmigan, and roasted one of them at once; then I tied up Aesop.

I lay on the dry ground as I ate. It was quiet over the earth, just a gentle sighing of the wind and here and there the sound of birds. I lay and watched the branches waving gently in the breeze; a diligent little wind was bearing the pollen from twig to twig and filling each innocent blossom; the whole forest was in ecstasy. A little green caterpillar loops its way along a branch, without pause, as though it could not rest. It scarcely sees anything, although it has eyes; often it rears up and feels the air for something to catch hold of; it looks like a bit of green thread slowly stitching a seam along the branch. Perhaps by evening it will have arrived where it wants to be.

Still quiet, I get up and walk, sit down and get up again. It is about four o'clock; when it is six I shall start for home and see if I meet anybody. I still have two hours and I am already a bit restless and brush the heather and the moss from my clothes. I know well the places I pass, trees and stones stand there as before in their solitude, the leaves rustle under my feet. The monotonous sighing of the wind and the familiar trees and stones mean much to me; I feel a strange sense of gratitude, everything reaches out towards me, blends with me, I love all things. I take up a dry twig and hold it in my hand as I sit there and think my own thoughts; the twig is nearly rotten, its meagre bark distresses me, and pity steals through my heart. And when I get up to go, I do not fling away the twig but lay it down and stand and gaze fondly at it; finally, with moist eyes, I give it one last look before I forsake it.

Soon it is five o'clock. The sun shows me the wrong time; I have walked westwards the whole day and I am perhaps half an hour fast by my sun marks at the hut. I allow for all this; but all the same I still have an hour until six o'clock, so I get up again and walk a little further. And the leaves rustle under my feet. So another hour goes by.

I see below me the little river and the little mill which has lain ice-bound during the winter, and I stop. The mill is working, its noise pulls me up with a start, I stop at once. 'I have stayed out too long!' I say aloud. A pang goes right through me; I turn at once and set off for home, but all the time I know that I have stayed out too long. I begin to walk faster, to run. Aesop understands there is something amiss, he tugs at the leash, drags me along, whimpering excitedly. The dry leaves spurt from under our feet.

But when we came down to the edge of the forest, there was nobody there; no, everything was quiet, there was nobody there.

'There is nobody here,' I say to myself. And yet I had not expected it to be otherwise.

I did not stand there for long, but went, drawn by all my thoughts, straight past my hut, down to Sirilund, with Aesop and my bag and my gun and all my paraphernalia.

Herr Mack received me with the greatest friendliness and invited me to supper.

# 7

I BELIEVE I can read something of the minds of those about me; perhaps it is not so. Oh, on my good days I feel as though I can gaze deep into the minds of others, even though I am not particularly clever in other ways. We sit in a room, a few men, a few women and I, and I seem to see what goes on within these people and what they think of me. I read something into every fleeting glance of their eyes; at times the blood rises to their cheeks and they flush, at other times they pretend to be looking elsewhere, but they observe me out of the corners of their eyes. There I sit watching it all, and nobody suspects that I see through every mind. For many years I have supposed that I could read in the minds of everyone I met. Perhaps it is not so. . . .

I stayed the whole evening in Herr Mack's sitting-room. I could have left again at once, I was not really interested in sitting on there; but had I not come precisely because all my thoughts had drawn me there? Could I then really leave at once? After we had eaten, we played whist and drank toddy; I sat with my back to the rest of the room and with my head bowed; Edvarda went in and out behind me. The Doctor had travelled home.

Herr Mack showed me the arrangement of his new lamps, the first paraffin lamps to come up north, magnificent things on heavy leaden feet; he lit them every evening himself to avoid accidents. Once or twice he spoke of his grandfather, the Consul: 'My grandfather, Consul Mack, received this clasp from King Carl Johan's own hands,' he said, and pointed to his diamond clasp. His wife was dead, he showed me a painting of her in one of the smaller rooms, a distinguished-looking woman with a lace bonnet and a polite smile. In the same room stood a book-case with even some old French books that looked as though they were inherited; they had fine, gilt bindings and many owners had written their names in them. Among the books was a number of educational works; Herr Mack was a thinking man.

His two shop assistants had to be brought in for whist; they played slowly and uncertainly, counted up carefully but made mistakes all the same. One of them was helped by Edvarda.

I upset my glass; I rose unhappily.

'Oh dear, I have upset my glass!' I said.

Edvarda burst out laughing and said: 'Yes, we can see that well enough.'

They all assured me laughingly that there was no harm done. They gave me a towel to dry myself with and we continued playing. Soon it was eleven o'clock.

A vague feeling of displeasure shot through me

at Edvarda's laughter; I looked at her and thought that her face had become empty and unlovely. At last Herr Mack broke up the game on the pretext that the two assistants had to go to bed; and then he leant back in the sofa and began to talk about putting a sign up on his wharf, and asked my advice about it. What colour should he use? I was bored; without thinking I answered 'Black.' At once Herr Mack said the same: 'Black, just what I had thought myself. *Salt and Barrel Depot* in heavy black lettering, that is the most dignified. . . . Edvarda, aren't you going to bed yet?'

Edvarda rose, shook hands with us both, said 'Good night' and went. We sat on. We talked about the railway that had been completed last year, and about the first telegraph line. God knows when the first telegraph will come up north! Pause.

'You see,' said Herr Mack, 'I am gradually getting on in years, forty-six now, and my hair and beard are grey. Yes, I feel that I have aged a little. If you saw me during the day, you might think me still young; but when evening comes and I am alone, I begin to look my age. Then I sit here in this room and play Patience. It comes out all right with a bit of cheating. Ha! Ha!'

'It comes out with a bit of cheating?' I asked.

'Yes.'

And I fancied I could read in his eyes. . . .

He rose, strolled over to the window and looked

out; he stood with bent back, and his neck and throat were hairy. I got up as well. He turned and came towards me in his long pointed shoes; he stuck both thumbs in his waistcoat pockets and flapped his arms a little like wings, smiling at the same time. Then once again he offered to put a boat at my disposal and held out his hand.

'You must let me see you home,' he said and blew out the lamps. 'Yes, I shall enjoy a little stroll, it is not late yet.'

We went out.

He pointed up the road towards the smith's house and said: 'This way! This is the shortest.'

'No,' I answered, 'it is shorter round by the quayside.'

We argued the point a little without reaching agreement. I was convinced that I was right and I could not understand his insistence. At last he suggested that we should each go our own way and the one to get there first should wait at the hut.

We set off; he soon disappeared in the forest.

I walked at my usual pace and reckoned I should arrive at least five minutes before him. But when I reached the hut he was already standing there. He called out to me: 'There, you see! I always go that way, it really is the shortest.'

I looked at him in amazement; he was not warm and did not appear to have been running. He took his leave at once, thanked me for a pleasant evening and went back the same way he had come.

I stood there thinking: this is very curious! I ought to be a fair judge of distance and I have come both ways several times. My dear man, you are cheating again! Was it all a pretence?

I saw his back disappearing again into the forest.

The next moment I was following him, hurrying cautiously; I saw him wiping his face all the time and I was not so sure now that he had not been running. He now began to walk very slowly and I kept my eyes on him; he stopped at the smith's house. I dodged into hiding and I saw the door open and Herr Mack go into the house.

It was one o'clock; I could tell from the sea and from the grass.

# 8

A FEW days passed as best they might; my only friend was the forest and the great solitude. Dear God, I had never known such solitude as on the first of these days. It was full Spring; I found wintergreen and yarrow in the fields, and the chaffinches had arrived; I knew all the birds. Sometimes I took a couple of coins from my pocket and chinked them together to break the solitude. I thought: what if Diderik and Iselin came along!

Soon there began to be no night; the sun barely

dipped his face into the sea and then came up again, red, refreshed, as if he had been down to drink. How strangely affected I was sometimes these nights; no man would believe it. Was Pan sitting in a tree watching to see how I would act? And was his belly open; and was he crouching so that he seemed to sit and drink from his own belly? But all this he did just to keep one eye cocked on me; and the whole tree shook with his silent laughter when he saw all my thoughts running away with me. In the forest there was rustling everywhere; animals snuffled, birds called to each other, their cries filled the air. It was a year for Mayflies, their whirring mingled with that of the moths so that there was a sound as of whispering back and forth all over the forest. How much there was to hear! For three nights I did not sleep, I thought of Diderik and Iselin.

See, I thought, they might come. And Iselin would lure Diderik over to a tree and say: ' Stand here, Diderik, and watch, keep guard over Iselin; that hunter shall tie my shoe-lace.'

And I am that hunter and she will sign to me with her eyes so that I may understand. And when she comes, my heart understands all and it no longer beats, it booms. And she is naked under her dress from head to foot and I place my hand on her.

' Tie my shoe-lace! ' she says with flaming cheeks. And in a little while she whispers against my mouth, against my lips: 'Oh, you are not tying my shoe-lace, you my dearest heart, you are not tying . . . not tying my. . . .'

But the sun dips his face into the sea and comes up again, red, refreshed, as if he had been down to drink. And the air is filled with whispers.

An hour later she says against my mouth: 'Now I must leave you.'

And she waves back to me as she goes and her face is still flaming, her face is tender and ecstatic. Again she turns to me and waves.

But Diderik steps forth from the tree and says: 'Iselin, what were you doing? I saw you.'

She answers: 'Diderik, what did you see? I did nothing.'

'Iselin, I saw you do it,' he says again. 'I saw.'

Then her loud and happy laughter sounds through the forest and she walks away with him, exulting and sinful from head to foot. And where does she go? To the next one, a hunter in the forest.

It was midnight. Aesop had broken loose and was out hunting on his own; I heard him baying up in the hills and when I finally had him again it was one o'clock. A goatherd girl came along; she was knitting a stocking and humming and looking about her. But where was her flock? And what was she doing there in the forest at midnight? Nothing, nothing. Perhaps she was restive, perhaps just glad to be alive, what does it matter? I thought: she has heard Aesop barking and knows I am out in the forest.

When she came, I stood up and looked at her and saw how young and slender she was. Aesop also stood and looked at her.

'Where are you from?' I asked her.

'From the mill,' she answered.

But what could she have been doing at the mill so late at night?

'How is it that you dare to walk here in the forest so late at night,' I said, 'you who are so young and slender?'

She laughed and answered: 'I am not so young, I am nineteen.'

But she could not have been nineteen, I am convinced that she was lying and was only seventeen. But why did she lie and pretend to be older?

'Sit down,' I said, 'and tell me what they call you.'

And, blushing, she sat down by my side and said she was called Henriette.

I asked: 'Have you a sweetheart, Henriette, and has he ever embraced you?'

'Yes,' she answered with an embarrassed laugh.

'How many times already?'

She remains silent.

'How many times?' I repeated.

'Twice,' she said softly.

I drew her to me and asked: 'How did he embrace you? Did he do it like this?'

'Yes,' she whispered trembling.

Then it was four o'clock.

# 9

I HAD a conversation with Edvarda.

'It is going to rain soon,' I said.

'What is the time?' she asked.

I looked at the sun and answered: 'Nearly five.'

She asked: 'Can you tell that so exactly by the sun?'

'Yes,' I answered. 'I can.'

Pause.

'But when you cannot see the sun, how do you know the time then?'

'Then I go by other things. There is high tide and low tide, there is the grass that lies flat at a certain time, and the changing song of the birds. Some begin singing when others stop. And then I can tell the time by the flowers that close up in the afternoon, and by the leaves that are sometimes bright green and sometimes dark green. Apart from that I can sense what time it is.'

'I see,' she said.

I knew that rain would come and did not want

to keep Edvarda standing there any longer in the middle of the road; I touched my cap. But she stopped me suddenly with a new question, and I stayed. She blushed and asked me what I was really doing up here, why I went hunting, why this and why that? For I just shot what was absolutely necessary for food, I did not work Aesop very hard?

She blushed and looked meek. I realised that somebody had been talking about me and she had been listening; she was not speaking her own thoughts. She roused a feeling of sympathy in me, she looked so forlorn; I remembered that she had no mother; her thin arms gave her a neglected look. These things just came over me.

Well, I did not shoot to murder, I shot to live. I might need *one* grouse to-day, so I did not shoot two, but would shoot the other one to-morrow Why should I shoot more? I lived in the forest, I was a son of the forest. It was also the close season for ptarmigan and hare from the first of June, there was practically nothing more for me to shoot; well, then I would fish and live on fish. I would get a boat from her father and row out in that. I did not go hunting just to be able to shoot things but to enable me to live in the forest. It suited me there; I lay on the ground for my meals and did not have to sit bolt upright on a chair; I did not upset my glass. In the forest I did as I liked; I could lie on my back and shut my eyes if

I wanted to; I could also say what I wished there. Often you might want to say something, make a speech, and there in the forest it sounded like speech from the very depths of your heart. . . .

When I asked her if she understood that, she answered ' Yes! '

I continued to talk because her eyes were resting upon me.

' If only you knew all the things that I see out in the fields,' I said. ' In the winter I might be walking along and I perhaps see the marks of ptarmigan in the snow. Suddenly the tracks disappear, the birds have flown. But I can tell from the marks of the wings in which direction the birds have gone and in a short time I pick them up again. There is always something novel in that for me. Many a time in the autumn there are shooting stars to watch. Then I think in my solitude: what, was that a world in convulsions? A world disintegrating before my very eyes? And to think that I, in my life, have been granted the spectacle of a shooting star! But when the summer comes, perhaps there is a small living creature on every leaf; I can see that some have no wings, they can never get far, they must live and die on that little leaf where they came into the world. Imagine! Sometimes I see the blue fly. Well, all this does not sound very much; I don't know if you understand.'

' Yes, yes, I understand.'

' Well, and then at times I look at the grass and

the grass may be looking back at me, who knows?
I look at a single blade of grass, perhaps it is
trembling a little and that seems to me to mean
something. I think to myself: this blade of grass
stands here trembling. And if it is a fir tree I am
looking at, then perhaps it has a branch that also
makes me think a little. But sometimes I meet
people as well on the moors, that happens
occasionally.'

I looked at her; she stood, stooping and listening.
I hardly knew her again. She was so absorbed
that she forgot all about herself; she had become
ugly and stupid-looking, her lower lip hung slack.

' Yes, of course,' she said, and straightened up.

The first rain drops fell.

' It is raining,' I said then.

' Yes, imagine! It is raining,' she said, already
walking away.

I did not accompany her home; she went her
way alone whilst I hurried up to the hut. Some
minutes passed and it began to rain heavily. All
at once I heard someone come running after me;
I stop and see Edvarda. She was red from the
exertion and she smiled.

' I had forgotten,' she said breathlessly. ' About
the trip to the drying-grounds on the islands.
The Doctor is coming to-morrow; have you
time?'

' To-morrow? Yes, I have time.'

' I had forgotten,' she said and smiled.

As she went, I noticed the beautiful lean calves of her legs, they were wet far above the ankles. Her shoes were very worn.

## *10*

THERE is one day that I still remember well. It was the day my summer came. The sun began shining when it was still night and dried the wet ground for the morning. The air had become soft and fresh after the recent rain.

It was afternoon when I joined the party down at the landing stage. The water was perfectly calm, we heard talking and laughing coming from the island where the men and girls were busy with the fish. It was a happy afternoon.

Yes, wasn't it a happy afternoon! We had baskets of food and wine with us, a large party of people split up into two boats, young ladies in light frocks. I was so happy I hummed a little tune.

Sitting in the boat, I began wondering where all the young people were from. There were the daughters of the bailiff and the district surgeon, one or two governesses, and the ladies from the vicarage; I had never seen them before, they were strangers to me and yet they were as friendly to me as if we had known each other for years. I

committed several blunders; I had become un-
accustomed to being among people and often
addressed the young ladies as 'Du'; but it was
not held against me. Once I said 'Dear' or 'My
dear', but I was forgiven for that as well; they
simply pretended that I had not said it.

Herr Mack had an unstarched shirt on as usual,
with the diamond clasp. He seemed in excellent
spirits and called across to the other boat: 'Take care
of those baskets with the bottles, you crazy people!
Doctor, I hold you responsible for the bottles.'

'All right!' the Doctor shouted back. And just
those two shouts over the water from one boat to
another sounded to me so festive and merry.

Edvarda was wearing the same dress as on the
day before, as though she did not have another or
else did not want to change it. She wore the same
shoes too. I thought her hands were not quite
clean; but she had a brand new hat on with a
feather in it. She had brought her dyed jacket
with her to sit on.

At Herr Mack's request I fired a salute as we
stepped ashore—two shots, both barrels, whereupon
there were shouts and cheers. We rambled up
over the island, the workers greeted us and Herr
Mack stopped to speak to his employees. We
found daisies and buttercups and put them in our
button-holes; some of us found bluebells.

And masses of sea birds chattered and screamed
in the air and on the beach.

We stopped at a patch of grass where there were a few stunted birches all white in the bark; the baskets were unpacked, and Herr Mack uncorked the bottles. Light dresses, blue eyes, the ring of glasses, the sea, the white sails. We all sang a little.

Cheeks grew flushed.

AN hour later, my thoughts are full of joy. Even little things affect me: a veil flutters on a hat, a lock of hair comes undone, two eyes close with laughter—and I am moved. Oh, this day, this day!

'I hear you have such an amusing little hut, Lieutenant.'

'Yes, a nest, but so after my own heart! You must come and visit me one day. There's nothing like it anywhere. And there is an enormous forest behind it.'

A second girl joins us and says amicably: 'Haven't you been up north before?'

'No,' I answer. 'But already I know everything about it. At night I am face to face with the mountains, with the earth, and with the sun. But I shall not try to be bombastic. What a summer you have here! It bursts out in blossom one night when everyone is asleep, and in the morning there it is. I looked out of my window and saw it myself. I have two little windows.'

A third comes up. She is enchanting, with her attractive voice and small hands. How enchanting they all are! The third one says:

'Shall we exchange flowers? It brings good luck.'

'Yes,' I say and hold out my hand. 'Let us exchange flowers—and thank you. How pretty you are! You have a bewitching voice, I have been listening to it all the time.'

But she snatches her bluebells back again and says curtly: 'What are you thinking of? I did not mean you.'

She had not meant me! It hurt me that I had been mistaken; I wished myself home again, far away in my hut where only the wind spoke to me. 'I beg your pardon,' I said. 'Forgive me.' The other ladies look at one another, and move away so as not to humiliate me.

At this moment someone came quickly over to us; all saw her—it was Edvarda. She comes straight up to me, speaks to me, embraces me, clasps her arms around my neck and kisses me again and again on the lips. She keeps murmuring something but I do not hear what it is. I did not understand at all, my heart stood still, I was aware only of her ardent look. As she let me go, her little breast rose and fell. She stood there, with her brown face and brown neck, tall and slender, with flashing eyes and altogether heedless; everyone was looking at her. Once again I was fascinated by the curve of her dark eyebrows.

Dear God!—the girl had kissed me in front of everybody!

'What is it, Miss Edvarda?' I asked, and I hear my blood pounding, hear it somehow deep down in my throat, making it difficult for me to speak distinctly.

'Nothing,' she answers. 'I just wanted to, that's all. It's nothing.'

I take off my cap and mechanically brush back my hair as I stand looking at her. 'Nothing. . . .?' I thought.

The sound of Herr Mack's voice is heard from another part of the island; we cannot hear what he is saying from where we are. But I am glad to think that Herr Mack has seen nothing and knows nothing of this. It was good that he was somewhere else on the island just then. I feel relieved at this and step over to the others and say laughingly and with assumed nonchalance: 'May I beg you all to forgive me for my behaviour. Miss Edvarda wanted to exchange flowers with me, and I so far forgot myself that I offended her. I wish to beg her pardon and yours. Put yourselves in my position; I live quite alone, I am not accustomed to the society of ladies; besides which I have been drinking wine and I am not used to that either. Please be lenient with me.'

I laughed, pretending not to care about this bagatelle, in the hope that it might be forgotten; but inwardly I was grave. Nor had my words made any impression on Edvarda; she did not try to conceal anything or to obliterate the effect that her hasty action had made; on the contrary, she sat down close beside me and looked at me steadily. Now and then she said something to me. Later, when we were playing *Widow*, she said loudly: 'I want Lieutenant Glahn. I don't care to run after anyone else.'

'In Hell's name, girl, be quiet,' I whispered, and stamped my foot.

A look of surprise flew over her face; she made a pained grimace with her nose, and then smiled shyly. I was deeply moved; the forlorn expression of her eyes and of her whole thin figure was more than I could resist; I became fond of her and took her long, narrow hand in mine.

'Later,' I said. 'No more now. We can meet again to-morrow.'


## *II*


DURING the night I heard Aesop get up from his corner and growl; I heard him through my sleep, but as I happened to be dreaming of hunting just then, the growl fitted into the dream and I was not disturbed by it. When I stepped out of the hut at about two o'clock in the morning, there were footprints in the grass; someone had been there, and had gone first to one of the windows, then to the other. Further down the path they disappeared again.

S HE came towards me with fiery cheeks, her face radiant.

'Have you been waiting?' she asked. 'I was afraid you might have to wait.'

I had not been waiting; she had been there before me.

'Have you slept well?' I asked. I hardly knew what to talk about.

'No, I haven't. I have been awake,' she answered. And she told me she had not slept that night, but had sat in a chair and closed her eyes. And she had been out for a walk.

'Someone has been outside my hut during the night,' I said. 'I saw footprints in the grass this morning.'

And her face flushes, she takes my hand, there on the road, and does not answer. I look at her and ask: 'Was it you, perhaps?'

'Yes,' she answered, pressing close to me. 'It was me. I didn't wake you, did I? I went as quietly as I could. Yes, it was me. I was near you once more. I am so fond of you.'

## 12

EVERY day, every day I met her. I confess the truth, I was glad to meet her; yes, my heart took wings. It is two years ago this summer. Now I think of it only when I please; I now find the whole affair amusing and diverting. And as for the two green feathers, I shall explain them shortly.

There were several places where we met: at the mill, on the path, in my hut even; she came wherever I wanted. 'Hello!' she always called first, and I would answer 'Hello!'

'You are happy to-day, you are singing,' she says, and her eyes sparkle.

'Yes, I am happy,' I answer. 'You have a smudge of something on your shoulder there, it's dust, from the road perhaps. I want to kiss it—no, please, let me kiss it! Everything about you arouses tenderness in me, I am quite distracted by you. I didn't sleep last night.'

And that was true; for more than one night I had lain sleepless.

We walk side by side along the path.

'Tell me, am I behaving as you want me to?' she says. 'Perhaps I talk too much? No? But you must say what you think. Sometimes I tell myself that this can never go well. . . .'

' What can never go well?' I ask.

' This, us. It will not go well. You can believe me or not, but I am cold now. Something icy trickles down my spine the moment I come to you. From sheer happiness.'

' Yes, it is the same with me,' I answer. ' I also feel a shiver when I see you. But it will be all right. Anyway I'll slap you on the back a bit and warm you up.'

Reluctantly she lets me; I pat a little harder as a joke, and laugh; and I ask her whether that helps or not.

' Oh no, don't please thump me any more,' she says.

These few words! They sounded so helpless to me, the way she said them: ' Don't please thump. . . .'

We walked on along the path. Is she vexed with me because of my joke? I wondered and thought: we shall see. So I said:

' I've just remembered something. Once on a sleigh ride, a young lady took a silk scarf from her own neck and tied it around mine. That evening I said to her: I'll let you have your scarf back to-morrow when I have had it washed. No, she said, give it to me now, I want to keep it just as it is, just as you have worn it. So I gave it to her. Three years later I met this young lady again. The scarf? I said. She brought it out. It was wrapped in its paper, still not washed. I saw it myself.'

Edvarda glanced up at me.

'Yes, and what then?'

'Nothing, that was all,' I said. 'But I think it was rather nice.'

Pause.

'Where is she now?'

'Abroad.'

We spoke no more about it. But when it was time for her to go home, she said: 'Good night, then. Don't think about her any more, will you? I don't think about anyone but you.'

I believed her. I saw that she meant what she was saying, and it was for ever enough that she just thought of me. I went after her.

'Thank you, Edvarda,' I said. And then I added with all my heart: 'You are much too good for me, but I am grateful that you want me; God will reward you for that. I am not as splendid as many another you could have, but I am all yours, desperately yours, by my immortal soul. What are you thinking? There are tears in your eyes.'

'Nothing,' she answered. 'It sounded so strange that God would reward me. You say things like. . . . Oh, I love you so.'

And all at once she threw her arms around my neck, there in the middle of the way, and kissed me tempestuously.

When she had gone, I left the path and slipped into the concealment of the woods to be alone with my happiness. And then I ran quickly back again to see if anyone had noticed I had gone in there. But I saw nobody.

# 13

SUMMER nights and still water and endlessly still forests. Not a cry, not a footfall on the path, my heart was full as of dark wine.

Moths and other night insects came flying soundlessly in through my window, attracted by the glow from the hearth and by the smell of my roasted bird. They knock against the ceiling with a dull sound, whir past my ears so that a cold shiver passes through me, and settle on my white powder-horn on the wall. I watch them, they sit trembling and look at me; silk-moths and swift-moths and the rest. Some of them look to me like flying pansies.

I step outside the hut and listen. Nothing, not a sound, all things are asleep. The air is luminous with flying insects, myriads of buzzing wings. Over by the edge of the forest there is fern and monk's hood, the heather is in bloom and I love its small flowers. I thank God for every heather flower I have ever seen; they have been like tiny roses on my path and I weep for love of them. Somewhere near there are wild pinks; I cannot see them but I catch their scent.

But now, in the night hours of the forest, great white flowers have suddenly opened out, their chalices spread wide, and they breathe. And furry hawk-moths bury themselves in their petals and set the whole plant quivering. I go from flower to flower; they are in ecstasy, and I see their intoxication.

LIGHT footsteps, the sound of breathing, a happy 'Good evening.'

I reply and cast myself down on the way and embrace the two knees and the thin dress.

'Good evening, Edvarda,' I say again, faint with joy.

'How fond you must be of me,' she whispers.

'How grateful I must be,' I answer. 'You are mine and all day long my heart lies at peace within me thinking of you. You are the most beautiful creature on this earth, and I have kissed you. Sometimes I flush with joy to think that I have kissed you.'

'Why are you so fond of me just to-night?' she asks.

For numberless reasons; I had only to think of her to feel this way. That look from under the high arched brows, that lovely brown skin!

'How could I not love you?' I say. 'I go about thanking every tree that you are well and strong. Once at a ball there was a young lady who sat out dance after dance, and everybody left her sitting there alone. I did not know her, but her face impressed me and I bowed to her. Well? No, she shook her head. Won't you dance? I asked her. Can you imagine, she said, my father was so handsome and my mother a perfect beauty, and my father took my mother by storm. But I was born lame.'

Edvarda looked at me.

'Let us sit down.' she said.

We sat among the heather.

'Do you know what my friend says about you?' she began. 'She says you have an animal look, and when you look at her it makes her mad. It is as though you touched her, she says.'

I was seized with a strange joy when I heard that, not for my own sake but for Edvarda's, and I thought to myself: There is only one I care about, what does she say of the look in my eyes? I asked her:

'What friend was this?'

'I won't tell,' she said, 'but she was one of the party that went on the trip to the island.'

'Indeed!'

And then we spoke of other things.

'My father is going to Russia in a few days,' she said, 'and then I am going to give a party.

Have you been out to Korholmerne? We'll take a couple of baskets of wine, and the ladies from the Vicarage are coming again. Father has already given me the wine. Say you won't look at my friend like that again, will you? Please say you won't! Or else I shall not ask her to come.'

And without saying more, she threw herself passionately against my chest and looked at me, gazed into my face, breathing heavily. It was a dark look she gave me.

I rose abruptly and said in my confusion: ' So your father is going to Russia? '

' Why did you stand up so quickly? ' she asked.

' Because it is late, Edvarda,' I said. ' The white flowers are closing again now, the sun is rising, day is coming.'

I went with her through the forest and stood watching her as long as I could; far below, she turned and softly called good night. Then she disappeared. At the same moment, the blacksmith's door opened, a man with a white shirt front came out, looked about him, pulled his hat down further over his eyes, and took the road to Sirilund.

Edvarda's good night still sounded in my ears.

# *14*

HAPPINESS is intoxicating. I fire my gun and an unforgettable echo answers from hill to hill, drifts out over the sea and beats against some sleepy helmsman's ear. What am I happy about? A thought that comes to me, a memory, a sound in the forest, a person. I think of her, I close my eyes and stand still on the path and think of her; I count the minutes.

Now I am thirsty and I drink from the stream; now I walk up and down, counting a hundred paces this way and a hundred back again; it's late now, I think.

Has anything gone wrong? A month has passed, and a month is not a long time; there cannot be anything wrong! God knows this month has gone quickly. But the nights are often long; and I hit on the scheme of dipping my cap in the stream and letting it dry again, just to shorten the time while I wait.

I reckoned my time in nights. Sometimes there would be a night when Edvarda stayed away; once she stayed away for two nights. Two nights. There was nothing wrong, and yet I had the feeling that my happiness had passed its peak.

And had it not?

'Do you hear, Edvarda, how restless it is in the forest to-night? There is a ceaseless rustling in the undergrowth and the big leaves are trembling. Something is brewing perhaps; but that is not what I wanted to say. I hear a bird singing up in the hills, only a tom-tit; but he has been sitting there for two nights in the same place, calling and calling. Can you hear that same sound over and over again?'

'Yes, I can hear it. Why do you ask me that?'

'For no particular reason. He has been sitting there for two nights. I just wanted to tell you. . . . Thank you, thank you for coming this evening, dearest one! I sat here expecting you this evening or to-morrow and was looking forward to your coming.'

'And I too have been waiting. I think about you and I have collected the broken pieces of the glass you once upset and kept them; do you remember? Father went away last night, so there was a good reason for my not coming: so much packing to do and so many things to remind him of. I knew that you were waiting here in the forest, and I cried as I packed.'

But it is two nights, I thought, what was she doing on the first night? And why is there not so much joy in her eyes as before?

An hour passed. The bird up in the hills was silent, the forest lay dead. No, no, there was nothing wrong, everything was as before; she gave me her hand to say good night and looked at me with love in her eyes.

'To-morrow?' I said.

'No, not to-morrow,' she answered.

I did not ask why.

'To-morrow is our party,' she said with a laugh. 'I just wanted to give you a surprise, but you looked so miserable that I had to tell you at once. I was going to send you a written invitation.'

And my heart lightened immeasurably.

She went off, nodding farewell.

'One thing more,' I said, standing where I was. 'How long is it since you collected the broken glass and put it away?'

'How long?'

'Yes, is it perhaps a week ago, or a fortnight?'

'Why, maybe a fortnight. But why do you ask? No, I will tell you the truth: it was yesterday.'

She did it yesterday! It was no longer ago than yesterday she had been thinking of me! Everything was all right again now.

## 15

THE two boats lay on the water and we stepped aboard. We talked and we sang. Korholmerne lay out beyond the islands; it took some time to row there and on the way we chatted to one another from the boats. The Doctor was wearing light clothes, as were the ladies also. I had never seen him so genial before; he joined in the conversation, no longer merely the silent listener; I had a feeling that he had been drinking a little and was rather happy. When we landed, he claimed the attention of the party for a moment and bade us welcome. I thought to myself: so Edvarda has chosen him to be host!

He entertained the ladies in a most affable manner. To Edvarda he was courteous and kind, often fatherly and, as on so many previous occasions, somewhat pedantic. She mentioned a date and said at one point: 'I was born in thirty-eight'; and he said: 'Eighteen hundred and thirty-eight, I suppose you mean!' And if she had answered: 'No, in nineteen hundred and thirty-eight', he would have shown no embarrassment but merely corrected her and said: 'That surely cannot be right.' When I said anything myself, he did not disregard me but listened politely and attentively.

A young girl came up and shook hands with me; I did not know her again, could not remember her; and when I uttered a few surprised words, she laughed. It was one of the Dean's daughters; I had met her the day we went to the fish drying-grounds and had invited her to my hut. We talked together for a while.

An hour or two passes. I am a bit bored; I drink the wine they pour out for me and I mix with the others, chatting to everybody. Again I blunder once or twice, I am on insecure ground, and for the moment I forget how to respond to all the little civilities; I ramble on incoherently or else stand there dumb, and I begin to fret about it. Over there by the big rock we are using as a table the Doctor sits gesticulating.

'The soul! What is the soul?' he was saying. The Dean's daughter had accused him of being a free-thinker. Well, should a man not think freely? People imagined Hell as a sort of establishment underground with the Devil as managing director—or even a kind of monarch. He might mention the altar painting in the annex chapel: a Christ, with a few Jews and Jewesses, water into wine—all right. But Christ had a halo round his head. And what was a halo? A yellow hoop standing on three hairs!

Two of the ladies clasped their hands aghast, but

the Doctor saved himself and said jocularly:
'Yes, that sounds horrible, doesn't it? I must
admit it does. But if you repeat it to yourself
seven or eight times and think it over a little, it
soon sounds better. . . . Will the ladies do me the
honour of drinking with me?'

And he knelt down on the grass in front of the
two ladies; and instead of removing his hat and
laying it down before him, he held it high in the
air with his left hand and emptied his glass with
his head thrown back. I was quite carried away
by his self-assurance and would have drunk with
him myself if his glass had not been empty already.

Edvarda was following him with her eyes.
I stood near her and said: 'Shall we play *Widow*
again to-day?'

She gave a little start and got up.

'Don't forget we mustn't call each other *Du*
now,' she whispered.

But I had not said *Du* at all. I walked away
again.

Another hour passed. The day was dragging
on; I would have rowed home alone long ago if
there had been a third boat; Aesop lay tied up
in the hut, perhaps he was thinking of me.
Edvarda's thoughts were surely far away from me;
she was speaking of the joy of travelling to distant
places. Her cheeks flushed at the thought and
she made a slip in what she was saying: 'Nobody
would be more happier than I the day . . .'

' More happier . . .? ' said the Doctor.

' What? ' she asked.

' More happier! '

' I don't understand.'

' You said more happier, that's all.'

' Did I? I'm sorry. Nobody would be happier than I the day I found myself standing on board ship. Sometimes I long for places I don't even know of.'

She longed to be far away; she did not think of me. I stood there and saw from her face that she had forgotten me. Well, there was nothing more to be said; but I stood there myself and read it in her face. And the minutes went, painfully slowly. I asked several of the others whether we should not row back now; it was late, I said, and Aesop was tied up in the hut. But none of them wanted to go home.

I went over to the Dean's daughter for the third time; she must be the one who talked about my animal look, I thought. We drank together; she had restless eyes, they were never still; she kept looking at me and then looking away again, all the time.

' Tell me,' I began, ' don't you think that people in these parts are themselves like their short summer? That they are bewitching and ephemeral in the same way? '

I spoke loudly, very loudly, and deliberately so. I continued in a loud voice, and once again asked

the young lady to come one day and see my hut.
' God will bless you for it! ' I said in my distress;
and I was already thinking of finding a present to
give to her if she came. Perhaps my powder horn
was the only thing I had, I thought.

And she promised to come.

Edvarda sat with her face averted and let me talk
as much as I wanted. She listened to what the
others were saying and put in a word herself now
and again. The Doctor told fortunes, read the
young ladies' palms, and gave his tongue free
rein. He himself had small delicate hands and a
ring on one finger. I felt unwanted and sat down
for a while by myself on a stone. It was already
late in the afternoon. Here am I sitting all alone
on a stone, I said to myself, and the only person
that could make me move lets me sit. Not that
I care anyway.

A feeling of utter desolation took hold of me.
I could hear them talking behind me, and I heard
Edvarda laugh; at that I suddenly rose and walked
over to the company. My agitation ran away
with me.

' Just a moment,' I said. ' It occurred to me
while I was sitting over there that you might like
to see my fly-book.' And I took out my fly-book.
' Forgive me for not thinking of it earlier. Won't
you be so kind as to look through it? It would
give me great pleasure. You must see it all, you
will find both red and yellow flies in it.' And I

held my cap in my hand as I spoke. I realised I had taken off my cap and that this was a mistake, so I put it on again at once.

There was a moment of deep silence, and nobody took the book. At last the Doctor stretched out his hand for it and said politely: 'Thank you very much; yes, let's have a look at the things. It's always been a mystery to me how these flies are put together.'

'I make them myself,' I said, full of gratitude towards him. And at once I began to explain how it was done. It was so simple; I bought the feathers and the hooks; they were not particularly well fashioned, but then they were only for my own use. One could get flies ready-made in the shops, and they were lovely things.

Edvarda threw one careless glance at me and my book, and went on talking with her friends.

'Ah, here are the materials for them,' said the Doctor. 'Look at these beautiful feathers.'

Edvarda looked up.

'The green ones are beautiful,' she said. 'Let me see them, Doctor.'

'Keep them!' I exclaimed. 'Yes, do that! Do me this one favour to-day! Two green feathers! Please take them, let them be a memento.'

She looked at them and said: 'They are green or gold according to how one holds them in the sun. Thank you, if you really want me to have them.'

'Yes, I want you to have them,' I said.

She took the feathers.

Shortly after, the Doctor handed me back my book and thanked me. Then he stood up and asked if we should not be thinking soon of getting back.

I said: 'Yes, for God's sake! I have a dog tied up at home. You see, I have a dog, he is my friend; he is lying there thinking of me, and when I come he stands with his paws against the window to greet me. It has been a lovely day, now it is nearly over; let us row back. Thank you, everyone!'

I waited on the beach to see which boat Edvarda would choose and determined to go in the other. She at once called to me. I looked at her in astonishment; her face reddened; then she came up to me, held out her hand and said tenderly: 'Thank you for the feathers. . . . We are going in the same boat, aren't we?'

'If you want to,' I answered.

We got into the boat, she sat beside me on the same thwart and touched me with her knee. I looked at her, and she looked at me for a moment in return. I felt better when she touched me with her knee. I began to feel recompensed for that bitter day and to regain my good spirits, when she suddenly changed her position, turned her back on me and began talking to the Doctor, who was sitting at the tiller. For a full quarter of an hour

I simply did not exist for her. Then I did something that I regret and have not yet forgotten. Her shoe slipped off; I seized it and hurled it far out over the water—whether from joy at her nearness or from some urge to assert myself and remind her of my existence, I do not know. It all happened so quickly; I did not think, I just acted on an impulse. A cry went up from the ladies. I was as if paralysed by what I had done; but what good was that? It was done. The Doctor came to my aid; he shouted: 'Row!' and steered towards the shoe; and the next moment the oarsman had grasped it, just as it was filling with water and sinking below the surface. The man's arm was wet to the shoulder. There was a chorus of 'Hurrah!' from both boats because the shoe had been saved.

I was deeply ashamed, and felt my face change colour and twitch as I dried the shoe with my handkerchief. Edvarda took it from me without a word. Not until some time later did she say: 'I have never seen such a thing!'

'No, I don't suppose you have!' I said. I smiled and straightened myself; I pretended I had had some special reason for this prank, as if there had been something behind it all. But what could there be behind it? For the first time the Doctor looked at me with contempt.

A little time passed; the boats glided homewards; the feeling of awkwardness in the company disappeared, we sang, we were nearing the landing stage. Edvarda said: 'Do you know, we haven't drunk all the wine, there is still quite a lot left. We must have another party, a new party later on. We'll dance, we'll have a ball in the big room at home.'

When we were ashore I made an apology to Edvarda. 'How I long to be back in my hut,' I said. 'This has been a painful day.'

'Has it been a painful day for you, Lieutenant?'

'I mean,' I said evasively, 'I mean I have made it so unpleasant both for myself and for others. I threw your shoe into the water.'

'Yes, that was an extraordinary thing.'

'Forgive me,' I said.

# 16

HOW much worse could things become? I resolved to keep calm whatever happened, as God is my witness. Was it I who had forced myself on her in the first place? No, no, never! I merely happened to cross her path one fine day as she passed by. What a summer they had here in the north! Already the Mayflies had stopped flying around; and the people became more and more inexplicable, although the sun shone on them day and night. What were their blue eyes seeking? And what were they thinking behind their strange brows? Not that I cared about any of them, anyway. I took my rods and went fishing—two days, four days; but at night I lay in the hut with eyes wide open. . . .

'Edvarda, I haven't seen you for four days.'

'Four days, yes, that's right. Oh, but I have been so busy. Come and see.'

She led me into the big room. The tables had been moved out, the chairs set round the walls, everything shifted about; the chandelier, the stove and the walls had fantastic decorations of heather and some black material from the store. The piano stood in one corner.

These were her preparations for 'the Ball'.

'How do you like it?' she asked.

'It is wondrous,' I said.

We went out of the room. I said: 'Tell me, Edvarda, have you forgotten me altogether?'

'I don't understand you,' she answered in surprise. 'Didn't you see all the things I have been doing? Could I possibly have come to you?'

'No,' I agreed, 'perhaps you couldn't.' I was weary and faint from lack of sleep, my speech became empty and confused; I had felt unhappy the whole day. 'No, of course you couldn't come. What I was going to say . . . in a word, something has changed, there is something wrong. Yes, but I cannot see from your face what it is. How strange your brow is, Edvarda. I can see it now.'

'But I have not forgotten you,' she cried, blushing, and suddenly slipped her arm under mine.

'Well then, perhaps you have not forgotten me. But in that case I don't know what I am talking about. One or the other.'

'To-morrow you'll receive an invitation. You must dance with me. Oh! How we will dance!'

'Will you come a little way down the road with me?' I asked.

'Now? No, I can't do that,' she answered. 'The Doctor will be here any minute, he is going to help me with a few things; there is a good deal still to be done. Then you think the room will look all right like this? But don't you find. . . .'

A carriage stops outside.

'Is the Doctor coming by carriage to-day?' I ask.

'Yes, I sent someone down with a horse for him. I wanted to. . . .'

'Spare his bad foot, of course. Well, I must go now. Good day, Doctor! Glad to see you again. Still keeping well? I hope you will excuse my rushing off?'

At the bottom of the steps outside, I turned round. Edvarda was standing in the window watching me, holding the curtains aside with both hands to see; her look was thoughtful. An absurd feeling of joy runs through me, I hurry away from the house, lightfooted and my eyes dim; the gun was as light as a walking stick in my hand. If I could win her, I would become a good man, I thought. I reached the forest and thought again: if I could win her, I would serve her tirelessly as no other would, and even if she showed herself unworthy of me, if she took it into her head to demand impossibilities of me, still would I do all in my power and rejoice that she was mine. . . . I stopped and fell on my knees; and in humility and hope I licked the blades of grass by the side of the path; then I stood up again.

At last I began to feel almost sure. The change in her manner lately was just her way; she had stood looking after me as I went, stood in the window and followed me with her eyes until I was out of sight; what more could she do? My joy left me utterly confused; I was hungry and no longer felt it.


AESOP ran on ahead and a moment later began to bark. I looked up; a woman with a white scarf on her head was standing by the corner of the hut. It was Eva, the blacksmith's daughter.

'Hello, Eva!' I called.

She stood by the tall grey boulder, blushing all over her face and sucking one of her fingers.

'Is that you, Eva? What's the matter?' I asked.

'Aesop has bitten me,' she replied, and shyly lowered her eyes.

I looked at her finger. She had bitten it herself. A suspicion flashed through my mind, and I asked her: 'Have you been waiting here long?'

'No, not very long,' she answered.

And without either of us saying another word, I took her by the hand and led her into the hut.

# 17

I CAME from my usual fishing and arrived at the 'ball' with gun and bag—all I had done was to put on my best leather suit. It was late when I came to Sirilund; I heard them dancing inside. Then someone shouted: 'Here's the hunter, the Lieutenant!' A few of the young people crowded round me and wanted to see my catch; I had shot a couple of sea birds and caught a few haddock. Edvarda bade me welcome with a smile; she had been dancing and was flushed.

'The first dance with me,' she said.

And we danced. Nothing untoward happened; I became dizzy but I did not fall. My heavy boots made rather a lot of noise; I could hear what a noise it was myself, and I decided not to dance any more; I had even scratched the painted floor. But how glad I was that I had done nothing worse!

Herr Mack's two shop assistants were there,

being very scrupulous and earnest about their dancing. The Doctor took part eagerly in the set dances. Apart from these gentlemen there were also four quite young men, sons of certain church dignitaries and of the Dean and the district surgeon. A visiting commercial traveller had also come; he distinguished himself by his fine voice and he hummed in tune to the music; now and again he relieved the ladies at the piano.

I no longer remember how we passed the first hour or two, but of the later part of the night I remember everything. The sun shone red through the windows the whole time, and the sea birds slept. We had cakes and wine, we talked loudly and we sang; Edvarda's laugh rang fresh and carefree through the room. But why had she never a word for me now? I went over to where she was sitting, meaning to make some polite remark as well as I could; she was wearing a black dress, her confirmation dress perhaps, and it was now much too short, but it suited her when she danced, and I wanted to tell her so.

' That black dress. . . .' I began.

But she stood up, put an arm about one of her friends and walked away with her. This happened two or three times. All right, I thought to myself, there's nothing to be done! But then why should she stand and look sorrowfully after me from the window when I leave her? Well, that's her affair!

A lady asked me to dance. Edvarda was sitting

near, and I answered in a loud voice: 'No, I am going now.'

Edvarda looked at me quizzically, and said: 'Going? Oh no, you are not going.'

I started, and felt my teeth pressing into my lips. I got up.

'What you said then seems rather significant to me, Miss Edvarda,' I said darkly, and took a step or two towards the door.

The Doctor interposed himself, and Edvarda too came hurrying up.

'Please don't misunderstand me,' she said warmly. 'What I meant was that I hoped you would be the last to go, the very last. Besides, it is only one o'clock. . . . And listen,' she continued, her eyes sparkling, 'you gave our boatman five *daler* for saving my shoe from drowning. That was too high a price.' And she laughed heartily and looked around at all the others.

I stood open-mouthed, confused and helpless.

'It pleases you to jest,' I said. 'I have never given any boatman five *daler*.'

'Oh, haven't you indeed?' She opened the door to the kitchen and called the boatman in. 'Jacob, you remember our trip out to Korholmerne, when you saved my shoe that had fallen into the water?'

'Yes,' answered Jacob.

'And you received five *daler* for saving the shoe?'

'Yes, you gave me. . . .'

'All right! You can go!'

Why does she play a trick like that? I thought.
Is she trying to shame me? She won't succeed
with it; I am not going to blush for a thing like
that. And I said, loudly and distinctly: 'I must
point out to everyone here that this is either a
mistake or a lie. It has never once occurred to
me to give the boatman five *daler* for your shoe.
Perhaps I ought to have done so, but up to now
I have not.'

'Whereupon we continue the dance,' she said
with a frown. 'Why aren't we dancing?'

She owes me some explanation for this, I said
to myself, and I watched for an opportunity to
speak with her. She went into an ante-room and
I followed.

'Skaal!' I said, and raised my glass.

'I have nothing in my glass,' she answered
curtly.

And yet her glass was standing in front of her,
quite full.

'I thought that was your glass.'

'No, it is not mine,' she answered, and turned
with a pre-occupied air to her neighbour.

'I beg your pardon then,' I said.

Several of the guests had noticed this little scene.

My heart was hissing within me. I said in-
dignantly: 'But at least you owe me some
explanation. . . .'

She rose, took both my hands, and said urgently:
'But not to-day, not now. I am so miserable.

Oh God, why do you look at me like that? We were friends once. . . .'

Overwhelmed, I turned right about and rejoined the dancing.

Shortly afterwards, Edvarda came in as well; she went and stood by the piano where the commercial traveller was sitting playing a dance; her face at that moment was full of secret sorrow.

'I have never learnt to play,' she says, looking at me with dark eyes. 'If only I could!'

I could make no answer to this. But my heart went out to her once more, and I asked: 'Why are you suddenly so unhappy, Edvarda? If only you knew how it grieves me.'

'I don't know why,' she said. 'It's everything, perhaps. If only these people would go now, all of them. No, not you—remember you must be the last to leave.'

And again I brightened at these words, and my eyes saw the light again in the sun-filled room. The Dean's daughter came over and began talking to me; I wished her far, far away, and answered her in monosyllables. I deliberately did not look at her, since she had spoken about my animal look. She turned to Edvarda, and told her how somewhere abroad a man had once pursued her in the street, in Riga I think it was.

'He kept following me for street after street and smiling at me,' she said.

'Was he blind then?' I broke out, thinking it

74

would please Edvarda. And I shrugged my shoulders as well.

The young lady understood my rudeness at once, and answered: 'He certainly must have been, to run after anyone as old and ugly as me.'

But I gained no thanks from Edvarda; she drew her friend away, they whispered together and shook their heads. After that, I was left strictly to myself.

Another hour passes; out on the reefs, the sea birds begin to wake, and the sound of their cries reaches us through the open windows. A spasm of joy went through me when I heard these early morning cries and I longed to be out on the islands myself. . . .

The Doctor had once again found his good humour and attracted everyone's attention. The ladies never tired of his company. Can that be my rival? I thought, and I thought also of his lame leg and pitiable figure. He had acquired a new and witty oath, he said 'Death and Torment,' and every time he used that comical expression I laughed aloud. I felt in my misery that I wanted to give this man every advantage I could since he was my rival. I let it be Doctor here and Doctor there, and shouted: 'Listen to what the Doctor is saying!' and I forced myself to roar with laughter at the things he said.

'I love this world,' said the Doctor. 'I cling to life tooth and nail. And when I die, then I hope to find some little spot in eternity directly above London or Paris, so that I can hear the blare of the can-can of humanity all the time, all the time.'

'Splendid!' I cry, and choke with laughter, although I am not at all drunk.

Edvarda too seemed delighted.

When the guests were leaving, I slipped into the little ante-room and sat down to wait. I heard one after another saying good-bye on the step outside; the Doctor also took his leave and went. Soon all the voices died away. My heart beat violently as I waited.

Edvarda came in again. When she saw me, she stood a moment in surprise; then she said smiling: 'Oh, it is you there! It was kind of you to wait until the last. Now I am dead tired.'

She remained standing.

Rising, I said: 'You will want to rest now. I hope your feeling of depression has passed, Edvarda. You were so sad just now, and it hurt me.'

'I will get over it when I have had some sleep.'

I had no more to say; I went to the door.

'Thank you for to-night,' she said, offering me her hand. And when she wanted to see me to the door, I tried to dissuade her.

'There is no need,' I said. 'Please don't trouble, I can find my way. . . .'

But she came with me all the same. She stood

in the passage waiting patiently while I found my cap, my gun and my bag. There was a walking stick in the corner; I saw it well enough, I stared at it and recognised it, it was the Doctor's. When she realised where I was looking, she grew red with embarrassment; it was clear from her face that she was innocent and knew nothing about the stick. A whole minute passes. At last a furious impatience possesses her and she says trembling: 'Your stick—don't forget your stick.'

And before my very eyes she hands me the Doctor's stick.

I looked at her; she was still holding out the stick, her hand trembled. To put an end to it all, I took the stick and placed it back in the corner. I said: 'This is the Doctor's stick. I can't understand how a lame man could forget his stick.'

'You and your lame man!' she cried bitterly, and took a step towards me. 'You are not lame, no; but even if you were, you couldn't compare with him; no, you couldn't, you could never compare with him. There!'

I sought for some answer, but my mind was suddenly blank; I was silent. With a deep bow, I retreated out through the door and on to the steps. There I stood for a moment, staring straight in front of me, then I wandered away.

So, he has forgotten his stick, I thought, and he will come back this way to fetch it. He did not want to let *me* be the last to leave the house. . . .

I strolled quite slowly along the way, looking
about me, and stopped by the edge of the forest.
At last, after half an hour's waiting, the Doctor
came walking along towards me; he had seen me
and was walking quickly. Before he had time to
speak, I lifted my cap; I wanted to test him. He
raised his hat also. I walked straight up to him and
said: 'I gave no greeting.'

He took a step back and stared at me.

'You gave no greeting . . .?'

'No,' I said.

Pause.

'Why, it is all the same to me what you did,'
he said, turning pale. 'I was going to fetch my
stick. I forgot it.'

I had nothing to say to this; but I took my
revenge another way; I held out my gun in front
of him as though he were a dog, and said: 'Up!'

And I whistled and coaxed him to jump over it.

For a moment he battled with himself; his face
changed expression in the strangest ways, he
pressed his lips together and stared fixedly at the
ground. All of a sudden he looked at me sharply;
a half-smile lit his features, and he said: 'Why are
you really doing all this?'

I did not answer, but his words affected me.

Suddenly he held out his hand and said gently:
'There is something wrong with you. If you will
tell me what it is, perhaps. . . .'

Shame and despair quite overwhelmed me; his

calm words threw me off balance. I wanted to make it up to him again, I put my arm around him and exclaimed: 'Listen, you must forgive me! No, what could there be wrong with me? There is nothing wrong, I don't need your help. You are looking for Edvarda, perhaps? You will find her at home. But hurry, or she will have gone to bed by the time you get there; she was very tired, I saw that myself. This is the best I can tell you; it is true, you will find her at home—go on!'

And I turned and hurried away from him, strode swiftly through the woods and back to the hut.

For a while I sat there on the bed just as I had come in, with my bag over my shoulder and my gun in my hand. Strange thoughts took shape in my mind. Why had I given myself away like that to the Doctor? I was furious that I should have put my arm around him and looked at him with tears in my eyes; he would gloat over it, I thought; perhaps at that very moment he was sitting smirking to Edvarda about it. He had left his stick in the passage. Yes, even if I were lame, I couldn't compare with the Doctor, I could never compare with him—those were her very words. . . .

I go and stand in the middle of the floor, cock my gun, place the muzzle against my left instep and pull the trigger. The shot passes through the middle of my foot and bores into the floor. Aesop gives a short terrified bark.

Shortly afterwards there is a knock at the door.

It was the Doctor.

'Forgive me if I disturb you,' he began. 'You went away so suddenly, I thought there could be no harm in our having a little chat together. Smell of powder, isn't there?'

He was completely sober.

'Did you see Edvarda? Did you get your stick?' I asked.

'I found my stick. But Edvarda had gone to bed. . . . What's that? Heavens, man, you're bleeding!'

'No, hardly at all. I was just putting away my gun and it went off; it's nothing. But why the devil should I have to sit here and give you an account of all this? . . . So you got your stick?'

He was staring fixedly at my torn boot and the trickle of blood. With a quick movement he put down his stick and removed his gloves.

'Sit still—we must have that boot off. I thought it was a shot I heard.'

# 18

HOW I later regretted that mad shot! The whole affair was not worth it, and it served no purpose; it just kept me confined to the hut for several weeks. I still remember quite clearly all the irritations and annoyances it brought; my washerwoman had to come every day and practically live in the hut, attending to the housekeeping and doing the shopping. That went on for several weeks. Ah, well!

One day the Doctor began to talk about Edvarda. I heard her name, heard what she had said and done, and it was no longer of great importance to me now; it was as though he spoke of some remote and irrelevant thing. How quickly one can forget, I thought to myself with surprise.

'Well, and what do you think of Edvarda yourself, since you ask? I, to tell the truth, have not thought of her for weeks. Wait a moment, it occurs to me that there was something between you two, you were so often together. You acted as host once when we had a day out on the islands, and she was hostess. Don't deny it, Doctor, there was something—a sort of understanding. No, for Heaven's sake, don't answer me. You owe me no explanation, I am not asking because I really want to know; let us talk of something else if you like. When can I get about again?'

I sat there thinking of what I had said. Why in my innermost heart was I afraid that the Doctor might speak out? What was Edvarda to me? I had forgotten her.

Later the conversation turned to Edvarda again, and again I interrupted the Doctor—God knows what it was that I dreaded to hear.

'Why do you interrupt me?' he asked. 'Can't you bear to hear me speak her name?'

'Tell me,' I said, 'what is your real opinion of Miss Edvarda? I should be interested to know.'

He looked at me suspiciously.

'My real opinion?'

'Perhaps you have something new to tell me to-day. Perhaps you have proposed after all and been accepted. Can I congratulate you? No? But who the devil's going to believe you, eh? Ha! Ha!'

'So it was that you were afraid of!'

'Afraid of? My dear Doctor!'

Pause.

'No,' he said, 'I have not proposed or anything like that. But you have perhaps. One does not propose to Edvarda—she takes him who pleases her most. Do you imagine that she is just a peasant lass? She is a child that has been spared the rod too much; and she is a woman of many whims. Cold? No fear of that! Warm? Ice, I tell you. What is she then? A little girl of sixteen or seventeen, isn't that so? But just try to make an impression on that chit of a girl and she will mock all your efforts. Even her father can do nothing with her; ostensibly she does what he says, but actually she is the one in command. She says that you have·an animal look. . . .'

'You are wrong. It was someone else who said that.'

'Someone else? Who?'

'I don't know. One of her friends. No, it was not Edvarda who said that. But wait a moment, perhaps it really is Edvarda herself. . . .'

'When you look at her, it has such and such an effect on her, she keeps on saying. But do you think that takes you one hair's-breadth nearer? Not a bit! Go on looking at her, don't spare your glances; but as soon as she realises that you are gazing at her, she will say to herself: Look! There's that man standing there, looking at me and thinking he has won the day. And with a single glance or a bleak word she will have you a hundred miles away. Do you think I don't know her? How old do you suppose she is?'

'Surely she was born in 'thirty-eight?'

'A lie. I looked it up, out of curiosity. She is twenty, although she might well pass for fifteen. She is not a happy soul; there is a lot of conflict in that little head of hers. When she stands looking out at the mountains and the sea, and her mouth becomes drawn here, and is twisted in pain there, then she is unhappy; but she is too proud and too obstinate to cry. She is really quite romantic, she has a powerful imagination; she waits for her prince. What was that about a certain five *daler* note you were supposed to have given to somebody?'

'A joke; it was nothing. . . .'

'Oh, but it was something. She did much the same sort of thing with me once. It was a year ago. We were on board the mail boat while it was lying here in the harbour. It was cold and raining. A woman with a little child sits freezing on deck. Edvarda asks her: Aren't you cold? Yes, she was cold. Isn't the baby cold as well? Yes, the child was cold as well. Why don't you go in the cabin? asks Edvarda. I have only paid steerage, says the woman. Edvarda looks at me. The woman has only a steerage ticket, she says. What am I supposed to do about it, I say to myself. But I understand Edvarda's look. I am not a rich man, I have worked my way up from nothing and I look twice at my money before I spend it. So I move away from the woman and I think: if she must be paid for, let Edvarda pay for her herself; she and her father are better off than I. And, sure enough, Edvarda paid herself. She is wonderful in that way, her heart is in the right place. But as truly as I am sitting here, she expected me to pay for a cabin for the woman and her child; I could see it

in her eyes. And what happened after that?
The woman got up and thanked her for her kindness. Don't thank me, thank the gentleman over
there, says Edvarda, and calmly points at me.
What do you think of that? I hear the woman
thanking me as well, but I don't know what to
say, all I can do is to let things take their course.
That is just one side of her; but I could tell you
a great deal more. And as for the five *daler* for
the boatman, she gave him the money herself. If
you had done it, she would have thrown her arms
around your neck. You would have been the
great man committing extravagant follies for the
sake of a worn-out shoe; that conformed to her
ideas; she had intended that for you. And
because you did not do it, she did it herself in your
name. That is her way—irrational and calculating
at the same time.'

' Can no one win her, then? '

' She ought to be taken in hand,' said the Doctor
evasively. ' She is given too much rope; it is
quite wrong, she can do anything that she wants,
and win whenever she pleases. People respond
to her, nobody shows her indifference; there is
always someone at hand for her to work her charms
on. Have you noticed how I treat her? Like a
schoolgirl, a child; I order her about, criticise
what she says, watch my chance to drive her into a
corner. Don't you think she understands? Oh,
she is stiff and proud, it wounds her every time;

but she is also too proud to show it. But you have to treat her like that. When you came I had already been training her like that for a year, and it was beginning to show results; she cried with pain and vexation; she was becoming a more reasonable being. Then you came and spoilt it all. That's the way it is; one lets her go and another takes her on again; after you there will be a third, I suppose—who knows?'

Oh, I thought, the Doctor wants revenge for something! And I said: 'Tell me then, Doctor, why have you gone to all this trouble and inconvenience to let me know this? Do you want me to help you discipline her?'

'And then she is as fiery as a volcano,' he went on without paying any attention to my question. 'You asked me if anybody could ever win her? Certainly, why not? She is waiting for her prince, but he has not yet come; again and again she finds she is mistaken, she thought that you were the prince, especially since you had an animal look. Ha! Ha! You know, Lieutenant, you should really have brought your uniform with you. Now that would have counted for something. Why shouldn't somebody win her? I have seen her wring her hands for someone who might come and take her, lead her away, rule over her body and soul. Yes! But he must come from outside, appear suddenly one day as a being apart. I have a suspicion that Herr Mack is out on an expedition;

there is very likely something behind this journey of his. Once before he went away like this, and when he returned there was a man with him.'

'There was a man with him?'

'Oh, but he was not suitable,' said the Doctor with a wry laugh. 'He was a man of about my own age and he also limped as I do. He was not the prince.'

'And where did he go?' I asked, looking fixedly at him.

'Where did he go? From here? I don't know,' he answered in confusion. 'Well, well, we have been talking much too long about this. You'll be able to get about on that foot of yours in about a week. Good-bye!'

# 19

I HEAR a woman's voice outside the hut; the blood rushes to my head; it is Edvarda's voice:
'Glahn! Glahn is ill, I hear?'

And my washerwoman answers outside the door: 'He is almost well again.'

That 'Glahn! Glahn!' went through every nerve and bone in my body; twice she spoke my name, and it touched me; her voice was clear and vibrant.

She opened the door without knocking, stepped hurriedly in and looked at me. Suddenly I felt it was like the old days again; she was wearing her dyed jacket, with her apron tied low over her hips to accentuate the length of her body. I took in everything at one glance; the way she looked at me, her brown face with the high arch of her eyebrows, the strangely tender look of her hands, everything affected me so deeply, it left me confused. I have kissed *her*, I thought to myself.

I got up and remained standing.

'You get up, you are standing,' she said. 'Do sit down, your foot is hurt, you shot yourself. Good God, how did it happen? I have only just heard about it. I thought all the time: where is Glahn? He never comes now. I knew nothing about it. You shot yourself, I hear, several weeks ago; and I had no idea of it. How are you now? You have become terribly pale, I hardly recognise you. And your foot? Will it leave you lame? The Doctor says you will not be lame. Oh, I am so very happy for you that you are not going to be lame; I thank God for it. I hope you forgive me for coming like this; I ran rather than walked. . . .'

She leant towards me, she was close to me, I felt her breath on my face, I reached out my hands for her. At this she moved away. Her eyes were still moist.

'It happened like this,' I stammered. 'I wanted to put the gun away in the corner, but I was holding it wrongly, pointing down, like this; then suddenly I heard a shot. It was an accident.'

' An accident,' she said thoughtfully, and nodded. ' Let me see, it is the left foot—but why the left particularly? Yes, of course, an accident. . . .'

' Yes, an accident,' I interrupted her. ' How can I tell why it should have been the left foot? You can see for yourself, I held the gun like this, so it couldn't very well have been the right foot. Yes, it was not very pleasant.'

She looked at me reflectively.

' At any rate, you are recovering well,' she said, and looked about in the hut. ' Why did you not send the woman down to us for food? What have you been living on?'

We talked together for a few minutes more. I said: ' When you came, there was sympathy in your face and your eyes shone, you gave me your hand. Now your eyes are indifferent again. Am I mistaken?'

Pause.

' One cannot always be the same. . . .'

' Tell me just this once,' I said. ' What have I said or done this time for instance to displease you? It could serve as a guide for me in the future.'

She looked out of the window, towards the distant horizon; she stood and looked pensively before her and answered me without turning around: ' Nothing, Glahn. One has one's own thoughts sometimes. Are you disturbed now?

Do not forget, some give little, and it is much for them, others give all, and it costs them no effort; who then has given most? You have become melancholy while you have been ill. How did we come to speak about this?' Suddenly she looks at me, her face lights up with joy, and she says: 'But now get well again quickly. We shall be seeing each other.'

With that, she held out her hand.

And now it entered my head not to take her hand. I stood up, put my hands behind my back and bowed deeply; by this I meant to thank her for her kindness in coming to visit me.

'Forgive me if I cannot accompany you,' I said.

When she had gone, I sat down again to think about it all. I wrote a letter and asked for my uniform to be sent.

## 20

THE first day in the forest.

I was happy and languid; all creatures came near and regarded me, insects sat on the trees, and beetles crawled on the path. Well met! I thought. The mood of the forest suffused my senses through and through; I wept for love of all things, and was utterly happy, I yielded myself up in thanksgiving. You good forest, my home, God's peace, shall I tell you from my heart. . . . I stop, turn in all directions and, weeping, call birds, trees, stones, grass and ants by name, I look about and name them each in turn. I look up to the hills and think: 'Yes, now I am coming!' as if in response to a call. High up there dwells the dwarf falcon—I knew of its nests. But the thought of the nesting falcons up in the hills sent my fancies far away.

About midday I rowed out and landed on a little island, out beyond the harbour. There were lilac-coloured flowers on long stalks that reached to my knees; I waded through strange vegetation, through raspberry bushes and coarse grasses; there were no animals there, perhaps no man had been there either. The sea foamed gently against the rocks, muffling me in a veil of sound; far up by the nesting rocks all the birds of the coast were flying and screaming. But the sea enclosed me on all sides as if in an embrace. Blessed be life and earth and sky, blessed be my enemies, in this hour I want to be merciful to my bitterest enemy, and tie the bands of his shoes.

A snatch of a sea-shanty carries across from one of Herr Mack's boats and my heart fills with sunlight at this familiar sound. I row back to the quay, make my way past the fishermen's cottages and so homewards. Day is ended; I have my meal, sharing my food with Aesop, and go again into the forest. A soft wind gently wafts against my face. 'A blessing on you,' I say to the winds

because they fan my face, ' a blessing on you; the
blood in my veins bows to you in gratitude.'
Aesop lays one paw on my knee.

Weariness comes over me and I fall asleep.


LULL! Lull! Bells ringing? Some miles out to
sea stands a mountain. I say two prayers,
one for my dog and one for myself, and we enter
the mountain. The gate slams behind us; I start
at the sound and wake.

Flaming red sky, the sun stands and stamps before
my eyes, the night, the horizon reverberates with
light. Aesop and I move into the shade. All is
quiet around us. ' No, we will sleep no more,'
I say to the dog, ' we will go hunting in the morning,
the red sun shines upon us, we did not enter the
mountain. . . .' And strange moods are born
within me and the blood rises to my head.

Excited but still weak, I feel that someone kisses
me, and the kiss lies on my lips. I look about me,
there is nobody there to see. There is a rustling
in the grass, it might be leaves falling to the ground,
it might be footsteps. A shudder passes through
the forest: that could be Iselin's breath, I think.
These are the woods where Iselin walked; here
she gave ear to the hunter's entreaties, in their
yellow boots, their green cloaks. She lived on her
estate, half a league from here; four generations
ago, she sat at her window and heard the sound

of the horn in the forest. Reindeer and wolf and bear were here, and the hunters were many, and all watched her grow and waited, each and every one, for her. One had seen her eyes, another had heard her voice; and one sleepless swain rose one night from his bed and drilled a hole through to Iselin's chamber and saw the white velvet of her body. When she was twelve, Dundas came. He was a Scot, he traded in fish and owned many ships. He had a son. When Iselin was sixteen, she saw for the first time the young Dundas. He was her first love. . . .

And such strange fancies pass before me, and my head grows heavy as I sit there; I close my eyes and feel again Iselin's kiss. ' Iselin, beloved of life, are you here? And have you hidden Diderik behind a tree?' . . . But heavier and heavier grows my head, and I float away on the waves of sleep.

Lull! Lull! A voice speaks, and it is as if the Seven Stars themselves were singing through my blood; it is the voice of Iselin:

Sleep! sleep! and I will tell you of my love while you sleep, and I will tell you of my first night. I remember it still, I forgot to bar my door; I was sixteen years old, it was spring and mild winds blew; Dundas came. It was like the swoop of an eagle's flight. I met him one morning, before the hunt; he was twenty-five and had journeyed in distant lands; he walked by my side in the garden; and when he touched me with his arm I began to love him. Two fever-red patches showed on his brow, and I could have kissed those two patches.

In the evening after the hunt, I went to seek him in the garden, and was afraid lest I should find him. I spoke his name softly to myself, and was afraid lest he should hear. Then he stepped forth from the bushes and whispered: 'To-night on the stroke of one!' And he was gone.

'On the stroke of one,' I say to myself, 'what was his meaning in that?' I do not understand. He surely meant that he was going away—but what is it to me when he goes?

And thus it was that I forgot to bar my door. . . .

One hour after midnight he enters.

'Was my door not barred?' I ask.

'I will bar it now,' he answers.

And he bars the door and shuts us in.

I feared the noise of his heavy boots. 'Do not wake my maid,' I said. And I feared also the creaking of the chair, and I said: 'No, do not sit on that chair for it creaks.'

'May I sit with you on the couch?' he asked.

'Yes,' I said.

But I only said that because the chair creaked.

We sat there on my couch; I moved away, and he moved nearer to me. I lowered my eyes.

'You are cold,' he said and took my hand.

Soon after, he said: ' How cold you are! ' and put his arm about me.

I grew warm in his arm. Thus we sit a short while. A cock crows.

' Did you hear? ' he said. ' A cock crew. Soon it will be morning.'

And he touched me and I was lost.

' If you are sure it was the cock that crew,' I stammered.

Again I saw the two fever-red patches on his brow, and I tried to rise. But then he held me back; I kissed the two enchanting patches and closed my eyes to him. . . .

Then the day came, already it was morning. I woke, and did not recognise the walls of my chamber; I got up and did not recognise my own little shoes; something was trembling within me. What is this that trembles within me? I thought, smiling. And what hour did the clock strike just now? I knew nothing, I remembered only that I had forgotten to bar my door.

My maid comes.

' Your flowers have had no water,' she says.

I had forgotten my flowers.

' You have crumpled your dress,' she continues.

Where can I have crumpled my dress? I ask myself, with a laughing heart. It must surely have been last night?

A carriage drives up to the gate.

' And your cat has had no milk,' says the maid.

But I forget my flowers, my dress and my cat, and ask: ' Is it Dundas who stops at the gate? Ask him to come to me at once, I await him, there was something . . . something. . . .' And I think: will he bar the door again when he comes?

He knocks. I open the door and bar it again myself, as a small service to him.

' Iselin! ' he cries, and kisses my lips a full minute long.

' I did not send for you,' I whisper to him.

' Did you not? ' he asks.

Then again I am wholly lost, and I answer: ' Yes, I did—I did send for you. I yearned so unutterably for you again. Stay here a little.'

And I closed my eyes for love of him. He did not let me go; I sank down and clung close to him.

' I thought I heard the cock crow again,' he said, listening.

But when I heard what he said, I broke in as swiftly as I could, and replied: ' No, how can you imagine that the cock crew again? I heard nothing crow.'

He kissed my breast.

' It was only the clucking of a hen,' I say at the last moment.

' Wait a little, I will bolt the door,' he said, and was about to rise.

But I held him back and whispered: ' It is bolted. . . .'

Then it was evening again and Dundas was gone.

Something golden trembled within me. I stood before the mirror, and two love-lorn eyes looked out at me, I felt something moving within me as I gazed, trembling, trembling round my heart. Dear God, I had never seen myself with those eyes before, and in a rapture of love I kissed my own lips in the mirror. . . .

And now I have told you of my first night, and of the morning and the evening that followed. Another time I shall tell you of Svend Herlufsen. Him I loved too; he lived three miles away, on the island you can see out there, and on calm summer nights I rowed out to him, because I loved him. I will also tell you of Stamer. He was a priest, and I loved him. I love all. . . .


THROUGH my sleep I hear a cock crow down at Sirilund.

'Did you hear, Iselin? The cock crew for us too!' I cry joyfully, and stretch out my arms. I wake. Aesop is already on his feet. 'Gone!' I say in burning sorrow, and I look about me. 'There is no one, no one here!' Fevered and excited, I go homewards. It is morning, and the cock is still crowing down in Sirilund.

By the hut stands a woman, stands Eva. She has a rope in her hand, she is going to gather firewood. The dawn of life lies over the young girl, her breast rises and falls, and the sun touches her with gold.

*97*

'You must not think . . .' she stammers.

'What must I not think, Eva?'

'I did not come this way with the idea of meeting you, I was just passing. . . .'

And she flushes deep red.

## 21

MY foot continued to give me discomfort and pain, it often itched at nights and kept me awake; sudden spasms would shoot through it, and when the weather changed I suffered a great deal with arthritis. It was like that for many days.

But it did not leave me lame.

The days passed.

Herr Mack had returned, and I was to know this very soon. He took my boat away, he made things very difficult for me, for it was still the close season and there was nothing I could shoot. But why did he rob me of the boat like that? Two of Herr Mack's workers from the quay had rowed out to sea with a stranger that morning.

I met the Doctor.

'My boat has been taken away,' I said.

'A stranger has come,' he said. 'They have to row him out to sea every day and bring him back again in the evening. He is investigating the sea bed.'

The newcomer was a Finn. Herr Mack had met him by chance on board ship; he was returning from Spitzbergen with a collection of shells and some samples of sea life; they called him Baron. He had been given a big room, together with a smaller one, in Herr Mack's house. He caused quite a stir.

I am short of meat, and I could ask Edvarda for something for this evening, I thought. I stroll down to Sirilund. At once I notice that Edvarda is wearing a new dress; she seems to have grown, her dress is very long.

'Excuse me if I don't get up,' she said curtly, and held out her hand.

'Yes, I'm afraid my daughter is not very well,' said Herr Mack. 'A cold, she hasn't been taking care of herself. . . . I presume you have come to find out about the boat? I shall have to lend you another one instead. It's not a new one, but as long as you keep baling. . . . The fact is, we now have a man of science in the house, and you will understand of course that a man like that. . . . He has no time to spare: works all day and comes home in the evening. Please don't go now before he returns, and then you'll see him, you'll be interested to meet him. Here's his card, coronet and all; he's a Baron. A charming man. I met him quite by chance.'

Aha, I thought, you are not being invited to supper. Well, thank heavens, I had only come to see how the land lay. I can go home again, I still have some fish left in the hut. There will be enough for a meal, I dare say. So that's that!

The Baron came in. A little man of about forty, with a long, narrow face, prominent cheekbones and a thin black beard. He had a sharp and penetrating glance, but he wore thick glasses. His cuff-links had the same five-pointed coronet on them as his card. He stooped a little, and his lean hands were blue-veined, but the nails were like yellow metal.

'Delighted to meet you, Lieutenant. Have you been here long, may I ask?'

'Several months.'

A pleasant man. Herr Mack asked him to tell us about his shells and his sea creatures, and this he did willingly; he told us about the kind of clay there was on Korholmerne, went into his room and fetched a sample of seaweed from the White Sea. He was constantly raising his right forefinger and shifting the thick gold-rimmed spectacles up and down on his nose. Herr Mack was greatly interested. An hour passed.

The Baron mentioned my accident, that unfortunate shot. Was I well again now? Really? He was pleased to hear it.

Who had been telling him about my accident, I wondered. I asked: 'From whom did you hear about my accident, Baron?'

'Oh, from . . . Who was it now? Miss Mack, I think. Isn't that right, Miss Mack?'

Edvarda flushed a fiery red.

I had come there so poor in spirit; for several days a dark despair had weighed me down, but at the stranger's last words a feeling of joy at once flickered through me. I did not look at Edvarda, but I thought: Thank you for speaking of me after all, for naming my name with your tongue, though it is for ever empty of meaning for you. Good night.

I took my leave. Edvarda still remained seated and excused herself for the sake of appearances by saying that she was unwell. She gave me her hand with indifference.

And Herr Mack stood chatting eagerly with the Baron. He was talking about his grandfather, the Consul: ' I don't know whether I told you before, Baron, that King Carl Johan pinned this clasp on my grandfather's breast with his own hands.'

I left the house; nobody saw me out. As I passed, I glanced in through the windows of the sitting-room and there stood Edvarda, tall, erect, holding the curtains apart with both hands and looking out. I neglected to bow to her. I forgot everything; a swirl of confusion overwhelmed me and bore me rapidly away.

' Wait, stop a moment! ' I said to myself when I had reached the forest. ' God in Heaven, but there must be an end to this! ' I suddenly felt hot with anger, and I groaned. Oh, I no longer had any pride in my heart; I had enjoyed Edvarda's

favour for a week at the most, and that was now
long past, and yet I could not reconcile myself to
it. From now on, my heart would cry to her:
' Dust, air, earth on my way, by God in Heaven . . .'

I arrived at the hut, took out the fish and had a
meal.

Here are you, burning out your life for the sake
of a little schoolgirl, and your nights are full of
desolate dreams. And a sultry wind enwraps your
head, a stale and musty wind. Whilst the sky
trembles with a marvellous blue, and the mountains
are calling. Come, Aesop, up!

## 22

A WEEK passed. I hired the blacksmith's boat
and fished for my food. Edvarda and the
Baron were always together in the evening when
he came home from the sea. I saw them once at
the mill. One evening they both came walking
past my hut; I drew back from the window and
gently closed the door, just in case. It left me
quite unmoved to see them together; I shrugged
my shoulders. Another evening I met them on
the path and we nodded to each other; I let the
Baron make the first move, whereupon I just lifted
a couple of fingers to my cap with deliberate dis-

courtesy. I walked calmly past them, looking at them with complete unconcern.

Another day passed.

How many long days had now gone by? A mood of depression was upon me, my heart brooded on things in silence; even the kindly grey boulder by the hut stood with a look of sorrow and despair as I went by. There was rain in the air; the heat was a thing that stood before me panting wherever I turned; there were twinges of arthritis in my left foot; I had seen one of Herr Mack's horses quivering in its harness that morning; all these things had a meaning for me as weather signs. It will be best to stock the house well with food while the weather holds, I thought.

I tied up Aesop, took my fishing tackle and my gun and went down to the quay. I was more than usually oppressed.

' When will the mail boat be in? ' I asked a fisherman.

' The mail boat? In three weeks time,' he answered.

' I am expecting my uniform,' I said.

Then I met one of Herr Mack's shop-assistants. I took his hand and said: ' Tell me, for Christ's sake, don't you play whist any more down in Sirilund? '

' Yes, often,' he answered.

Pause.

' I haven't been able to come lately,' I said.

I rowed out to my fishing grounds. The weather had turned very close, the gnats gathered in clouds, and I had to keep smoking all the time to protect myself. The haddock were biting, I fished with double hooks and landed a good catch. On the way back I shot a brace of guillemots.

When I reached the landing stage, the blacksmith was there, working. A thought struck me; I asked him:

'Coming home?'

'No,' he said, 'Herr Mack has given me a job to do here that will keep me till midnight.'

I nodded and thought to myself, that was good.

I took my fish and set off, taking the way past the blacksmith's house. Eva was at home alone.

'I have been longing for you with all my heart,' I said to her. And at the sight of her I was moved; she could hardly look straight at me, such was her amazement. 'I love your youth and your kind eyes,' I said. 'You must chastise me to-day because I have thought more of another than of you. Listen, I have come here just to look at you, it does me good, and I love you. Did you hear me calling you last night?'

'No,' she answered, terrified.

'I called Edvarda, Miss Edvarda, but it was you I meant; I woke myself up with it. Yes, it was you I meant; it was a slip of the tongue when I said Edvarda. But let us not talk about her any more.

My God, if you are not my best girl, Eva! Your lips are so red to-day. Your feet are prettier than Edvarda's—see for yourself.' And I lifted up her dress and showed her her own legs.

Joy such as I had never seen in her before lit up her face; she begins to turn away, but hesitates and then puts one arm about my neck.

A little time passes. We talk together, sitting all the while on a long bench and talking to one another of many things. I said: ' Can you believe it, Miss Edvarda has not learned to speak properly yet; she talks like a child and says " more happier "; I have heard her myself. Do you think she has a fine forehead? I don't. She has an evil forehead. And she doesn't wash her hands either.'

' But we weren't going to talk about her any more.'

' Quite right, I forgot.'

More time passes. I think of something and I fall silent.

' Why are your eyes wet? ' asks Eva.

' Actually she has a fine forehead,' I say, ' and her hands are always clean. It was only an accident that they were dirty once. I didn't mean to say more than that.' But then with clenched teeth I went on desperately: ' All the time I sit thinking of you, Eva. But it has just struck me you perhaps haven't heard what I am going to tell you now. The first time Edvarda saw Aesop, she said: Aesop? That's the name of a wise man, he was a Phrygian.

Isn't that ridiculous? She had read it in a book the same day, I'm sure of it.'

'Yes,' says Eva, 'but what about it?'

'And as far as I remember, she also talked about Aesop having Xanthus as a teacher. Haha!'

'Oh, yes.'

'Well, what the devil is the point of telling the company that Aesop had Xanthus as a teacher? I merely ask! Oh, you are not in the right mood to-day, Eva, or you would laugh yourself sick about it.'

'Yes, I think it is funny,' Eva says wonderingly, and forces a laugh. 'But I don't understand it as well as you do.'

I become silent and thoughtful, silent and thoughtful.

'Do you prefer us to sit here quietly and not talk?' asks Eva softly. There is a kindliness in her eyes, she runs her hand over my hair.

'You dear, dear soul,' I exclaim and hold her close to me. 'I am really pining away with love for you; I love you more and more; in the end you will come with me when I leave this place. You shall see. Could you come with me?'

'Yes,' she answers.

I can hardly catch that 'Yes', but I feel it in her breath, I sense it as something in her; we hold each other in a wild embrace, and desperately she gives herself to me.

AN hour later I kiss Eva good-bye and go. At the door I meet Herr Mack.

Herr Mack himself.

He gives a start, stares into the house, stands there on the doorstep and stares in. ' Ha,' he says, and he can say no more; he seems completely taken aback.

' You did not expect to find me here? ' I say, raising my cap.

Eva does not move.

Herr Mack composes himself, a strange air of confidence comes into his manner, and he answers: ' You are mistaken, it is precisely you I am looking for. I want to draw your attention to the fact that all shooting is prohibited within one mile of the bird breeding grounds between the first of April and the fifteenth of August. You shot two birds out at the island to-day, somebody saw you.'

' I shot two guillemots,' I said helplessly. It was at once clear to me that he was in the right.

' Two guillemots or two eider duck, it's all the same. You were within the prohibited area.'

' That I must admit,' I said. ' It didn't occur to me until now.'

' But it should have occurred to you.'

' I also fired off both barrels once, in May, at very nearly the same spot. It was the day of the trip to the islands. And it was done at your express request.'

'That is another matter,' Herr Mack answered shortly.

'Then you damned well know what you have to do, don't you?'

'Perfectly well,' he answered.

Eva held herself in readiness; when I went out she followed me. She had wrapped a scarf round her and she walked away from the house. I saw her take the way down towards the quay. Herr Mack walked back home.

I thought it over. What resourcefulness, to think up an excuse like that! And what piercing eyes! A shot, two shots, a couple of guillemot, a fine, a payment. And then the finish of everything, everything as far as Herr Mack and his house was concerned. Things really were going very neatly, so extraordinarily quickly. . . .

It had already begun to rain, large soft drops. The magpies flew close to the ground, and when I came home and turned Aesop loose, he ate the grass. The wind began to whine.

## 23

A MILE below me I see the sea. It is raining and I am up in the hills; an overhanging rock shelters me from the rain. I smoke my pipe, smoke one pipe after another, and every time I light up the tobacco curls up from the ash like little glowing worms. So is it also with the thoughts that teem in my head. In front of me on the ground lies a bundle of dry twigs, a shattered bird's nest. And as with that nest, so is it also with my soul.

I remember every minute detail of the events of that day and the next. Oh, how shamefully I was treated. . . .

I sit up here in the hills amidst the dreadful sound of the wind and the sea, with the seething and the wailing of wind and weather in my ears. Far out I can see fishing boats and other vessels with their sails reefed; there are people on board, bound no doubt for other places; and God knows, I think to myself, where all those lives are bound for. The sea flings itself up foaming into the air and tumbles, tumbles as if inhabited by great raging figures that flail their limbs and roar at one another. No, it is a pageant of ten thousand shrieking devils, ducking their heads between their shoulders and circling round, lashing the sea white with the tips of their wings. Far, far out lies a hidden reef; from that reef rises a white merman who shakes his head after some square-rigged boat that has sprung a leak and is sailing out to sea before the wind, ho! ho! out to sea, out to the desolate sea. . . .

I am glad to be alone, to know that none can see my eyes. I lean securely against the rock wall, knowing that no one can stand and watch me from behind. A bird swoops over the crest with a broken cry; at the same moment a boulder breaks loose not far away and rolls down into the sea. And I rest there for a while, quite still, sunk in repose; a warm and comfortable feeling steals over me as I sit so snug in my shelter while the rain pours down around me. I button up my jacket and thank God for the warmth of it. A little time passed. I fell asleep.

It is afternoon. I turn towards home; the rain is still falling. Then something unexpected happens. Edvarda stands on the path before me. She is soaking wet as if she has been out in the rain for a long time, but she smiles. Aha! I say to myself, and I feel my anger rising; I grip my gun fiercely as I walk towards her, even though she is smiling.

She is the first to call a greeting.

I wait until I have gone a few steps nearer before I say: 'I give you greeting, fair damosel.'

She is taken aback by my facetiousness. Oh, I

did not know what I was saying. She smiles timidly and looks at me.

'Have you been up on the fells to-day?' she asks. 'Look how wet you are. I have a scarf here, do please take it, I can spare it. . . . No, you don't want to have anything to do with me now!' And she lowers her eyes and shakes her head because I do not take her scarf.

'A scarf?' I answer, grinning mirthlessly in anger and astonishment. 'But I have a jacket here, do you want to borrow it? I can spare it. I wouldn't mind who I lent it to, so you need not worry about taking it. I would gladly have lent it to a fishwife.'

I could see she was anxious to know what I was going to say; she listened so intently that she let her mouth gape, and she looked quite ugly. There she stands with the scarf in her hand, a white silk scarf which she has taken from round her neck. I tear off my jacket as well.

'For heaven's sake put it on again,' she cries. 'You mustn't do that! Are you so angry with me? Oh please, put your jacket on again before you get soaked.'

I put on my jacket again.

'Where are you going?' I asked sullenly.

'Nowhere. . . . I can't understand why you should want to take your jacket off like that. . . .'

'What have you done with the Baron to-day?' I went on. 'Surely the Count can't be out at sea in weather like this?'

' Glahn, I just wanted to tell you something. . . .'

I interrupted her: ' May I ask you to convey my respects to the Duke? '

We look at each other. I am ready with further interruptions if she should as much as open her mouth. At last a look of pain passes over her face; I turn away and say: ' Seriously though, why don't you send the Prince about his business, Miss Edvarda? He is not the man for you. I can assure you he has been going about all these days wondering whether to make you his wife or not— and that surely cannot be good enough for you.'

' Please don't let us talk about that. Glahn, I have been thinking of you; you are the sort of man that takes his jacket off and gets wet through himself just to spare someone else. I have come to you. . . .'

I shrug my shoulders and continue: ' I suggest the Doctor instead. What can be said against him? A man in the prime of life, a brilliant mind. Consider it.'

' Listen to me for just a minute. . . .'

' My dog Aesop is waiting for me in the hut.'

I took off my cap, bowed to her again and said: ' I give you greeting, fair damosel.'

And with that I began to walk away.

She gave a cry: ' No, do not tear my heart from me. I came to you to-day, I waited for you up here, and I smiled when you came. Yesterday I was nearly out of my mind, my head was in a whirl and I was thinking all the time of you. To-day I was sitting at home and somebody came in, I did not look up but I knew who it was. I rowed half a mile yesterday, he said. Weren't you tired? I asked. Oh yes, very tired! And my hands are blistered, he replied, and was very distressed about them. And I thought: imagine, he is upset about a thing like that! After a little while he said: I heard whispering outside my window last night; it was your maid and one of the shop-assistants in intimate conversation. Yes, they are going to be married, I said. But this was two o'clock in the morning! And so? I said; and added: The night is their own. Then he pushed his gold-rimmed spectacles further on his nose and remarked: But all the same, in the middle of the night, don't you think it looks bad? I still didn't look up, and we sat like that for ten minutes. May I bring a shawl to put round your shoulders? he asked. No, thank you, I answered. If one but dared take your little hand! he said. I did not reply, my thoughts were elsewhere. He placed a little box on my lap, I opened it and found a brooch in it. On the brooch was a coronet and I counted ten jewels on it. . . . Glahn, I have the brooch with me now; would you like to see it? It is trampled to bits, just come and see how it is trampled to bits. . . . Well, and what am I supposed to do with this brooch? I asked. It is for your adornment, he answered. But I handed the brooch back to him and said: Leave me alone,

I think more of another. Which other? he asked.
One who hunts in the forest, I said. He gave me
only two pretty feathers as a souvenir; but take
your brooch back!—But he would not take the
brooch back. Then for the first time I looked at
him; his eyes were piercing. I will not take back
the brooch, do as you wish with it, stamp on it!
he said. I stood up and put the brooch under my
heel and trod on it. That was this morning. . . .
For hours I waited; and after lunch I went out.
He met me on the path. Where are you going? he
asked. To Glahn! I answered. To beg him not
to forget me. . . . Since one o'clock I have been
waiting here; I stood by a tree and saw you coming,
you looked like a god. I loved you—your figure,
your beard, your shoulders, loved everything about
you. . . . Now you are getting impatient, you want
to go, just want to walk away. I mean nothing to
you, you are not even looking at me. . . .'

I had stopped. When she finished speaking I
began to walk away again. I was worn out with
despair, and smiled; my heart was hard.

' Ah yes,' I said, and stopped again, ' you had
something to tell me, didn't you? '

This taunt made her weary of me.

' Did I have something to tell you? But I have
said it already, didn't you hear? No, nothing, I
have nothing more to tell you. . . .'

There is a strange tremor in her voice, but it
leaves me unmoved.

# 24

NEXT morning I find Edvarda standing outside the hut.

I had thought it all over during the night and made up my mind. Why should I let myself be dazzled any longer by this creature of moods, this fisher-lass, this ignorant person; had her name not sat long enough in my heart, sucking it dry? Enough of that! It occurred to me, moreover, that I had perhaps got closer to her precisely by treating her with scorn and indifference. Oh, how exquisitely I had mocked her; after she had made a long speech for several minutes, I had calmly said: 'Oh yes, didn't you have something to tell me?'

She was standing by the big boulder. She was greatly excited and was on the point of running towards me, she had already stretched out her arms, but she stopped and stood there wringing her hands. I took off my cap and silently bowed to her.

'There is just one thing that I want to ask you to-day, Glahn,' she said urgently. And I did not move, so as to hear what she was going to say. 'I hear you have been down to the blacksmith's house. It was one evening. Eva was alone in the house.'

I was taken unawares and answered: ' From whom have you received this information ? '

' I do not spy,' she cried. ' I heard it last night, my father told me. When I came home last night soaked through, my father said: You insulted the Baron to-day. No, I answered. Then he asked: Where have you been now? I answered: To see Glahn. And then my father told me.'

I struggle against my despair and say: ' What's more, Eva has also been here.'

' She has been here as well ? In the hut ? '

' Several times. I made her come in. We talked together.'

' Here as well! '

Pause. Don't weaken! I tell myself, and then say aloud: ' Since you are so kind as to meddle in my affairs, I'll not hold back either. Yesterday I suggested that you take the Doctor; have you thought it over? Because, of course, the Prince is really quite impossible.'

Anger flared up in her eyes.

' He is *not* impossible, I tell you! ' she cried passionately. ' No, he is a lot better than you; he can be in a house without breaking cups and glasses, and he leaves my shoes alone. Yes, he knows how to behave in company; but you are just ridiculous, I feel ashamed of you, you are intolerable—do you understand that? '

Her words struck deep; I bowed my head and said: ' You are right, I do not know very well how to behave among people. Be merciful; you don't understand me, I much prefer living in the forest, that is my joy. Here, where I am alone, it hurts no one that I am as I am; but when I meet others I have to strain every nerve to be as I should. In the last two years I have been so little in the society of others. . . .'

'With you one has constantly to be prepared for the worst,' she went on. 'In the end one grows weary of keeping an eye on you.'

How pitilessly she said that! I feel bitterly hurt, and I almost reel back before her vehemence. Edvarda had not finished yet, she added: 'Perhaps you could persuade Eva to look after you. What a pity she is married.'

'Eva? Did you say Eva was married?' I asked.

'Yes, married.'

'To whom is she married?'

'Surely you know that. She is married to the blacksmith.'

'Isn't she his daughter?'

'No, she is his wife. Do you think I am standing here telling you lies?'

I had not thought that at all, my astonishment was so great. I just stood there and thought: Eva married?

'So you have made a nice choice, haven't you?' says Edvarda.

There seemed to be no end to it all! I was trembling with fury, and said: 'But take the Doctor

as I told you. Listen to the advice of a friend;
that Prince of yours is a doddering old fool.' And
in my agitation I invented all sorts of things about
him, exaggerated his age, said he was bald and
almost totally blind, and declared that the only
reason he went about with that coronet on his shirt
studs was to boast of his rank. 'I do not value
his acquaintance,' I said. 'There is nothing about
him to distinguish him, he lacks fundamentals, he
is nothing.'

'But he *is* something, he *is* something,' she cried,
and her voice choked with anger. 'He is much
more than you think, you wild man of the woods!
But just you wait! Oh, he shall speak to you,
I shall ask him to. You don't believe that I love
him, but you'll see that you are wrong. I'll marry
him, I'll think of him night and day. Remember
what I am saying: I love him. Let Eva come,
hoho! God in heaven, let her come, it is so un-
speakably unimportant to me! But now I must
get away from here. . . .'

She began to walk down the path from the hut;
she took a few small hurried steps, then turned
round again, her face deathly pale, and moaned:
'And never come before my eyes again.'

# 25

THE leaves turned yellow, the potato plants had grown high and were in flower, the shooting season had come round again; I shot grouse, ptarmigan and hare; one day I shot an eagle. Calm, open sky, cool nights, many clear notes and well-loved sounds in the woods and fields. The earth was resting, great and peaceful. . . .

'I have heard nothing more about the two guillemots I shot,' I said to the Doctor.

'You can thank Edvarda for that,' he answered.

'I know; I heard her refuse to let anything come of it.'

'She shall get no thanks from me,' I said. . . .

Indian summer, Indian summer. The paths ran like ribbons in through the yellowing woods, every day a new star appeared, the moon showed dimly like a shadow, a shadow of gold dipped in silver. . . .

'God help you, Eva, are you really married?'

'Didn't you know that?'

'No, I didn't know.'

She pressed my hand in silence.

'God help you, child, what are we to do now?'

'Whatever you want. Perhaps you won't go

away just yet; I shall be happy as long as you are here.'

' No, Eva.'

' Yes, yes—just as long as you are here.'

She looks forlorn and presses my hand all the time.

' No, Eva, you must go! Never more! '

And nights pass and days come. It is already three days since this conversation. Eva comes along the path with a load. How much wood that child has carried home from the forest this summer!

' Put your load down, Eva, and let me see if your eyes are still as blue as ever.'

Her eyes were red.

' No, you must smile again, Eva! I can hold out no longer; I am yours, I am yours. . . .'

Evening. Eva is singing; I hear her singing and I feel a warm glow.

' You are singing to-night, Eva? '

' Yes, I am happy.'

And because she is smaller than I, she jumps up a little to put her arms round my neck.

' But Eva, your hands are torn and scratched! Oh, God, I wish you hadn't torn them so.'

' It doesn't matter.'

Her face is strangely radiant.

' Eva, have you spoken to Herr Mack? '

' Yes, once.'

' What did he say, and what did you say? '

' He is very hard on us now, he makes my husband work day and night down at the quay, and he gives me all sorts of work as well. He has ordered me to do man's work now.'

'Why does he do that?'

Eva looks down.

'Why does he do that, Eva?'

'Because I love you.'

'But how does he know that?'

'I told him.'

Pause.

'Oh, God, if only he weren't so harsh with you, Eva!'

'But it doesn't matter. It doesn't matter at all now.'

And the sound of her voice in the forest was like a little tremulous song.


AND the leaves turn yellower, autumn is approaching, more stars have appeared in the sky, and the moon now begins to look like a shadow of silver dipped in gold. There was no frost, nothing, only a cool stillness and an abundance of life in the forest. Every tree stood and thought. The berries were ripe.

Then came the twenty-second of August and the three Iron Nights.

## 26

THE first Iron Night.

At nine o'clock the sun goes down. A haze of darkness shrouds the earth, a few stars can be seen and two hours later a gleam of moonlight. I wander into the forest with my gun and my dog, kindle a fire, and the light from the flames shines in among the trunks of the firs. There is no frost.

The first of the Iron Nights! I say. And a strong and bewildering tremor of joy at time and place now runs through me, and I am strangely moved. . . .

'A toast, you men and beasts and birds, to the lonely night in the forest, in the forest! A toast to the dark and to God's murmuring in the trees, to the sweet, simple harmonies of silence upon my ear, to green leaf and yellow leaf! A toast to the sounds of life I hear, a sniffing snout in the grass, a dog snuffling over the ground! A rousing toast to the wild-cat crouching with throat to the ground and preparing to spring on a sparrow in the dark, in the dark! A toast to the merciful stillness over the earth, to the stars and the crescent moon, yes, to it and to them! . . .'

I stand up and listen. No one has heard me. I sit down again.

' I give thanks for the lonely night, for the hills, for the whispering of the darkness and the sea . . . it whispers within my heart. I give thanks for my life, for my breathing, for the grace of being alive to-night, for these things I give thanks from my heart! Listen in the east and listen in the west, but listen! That is the everlasting God! This stillness murmuring in my ear is the blood of all nature seething, is God weaving through the world and through me. I see a gossamer thread glistening in the fire's light, I hear the rowing of a boat in the harbour, the Northern lights rise against the northern sky. Oh, I give thanks by my immortal soul that it is I who am sitting here! . . .'

Quiet. A fir cone falls with a dull thud to the ground. I think: A fir cone fell! The moon is high, the fire flickers among the half-burnt embers, about to die. And I stroll home through the late night.

The second Iron Night; the same stillness and the mild weather. My soul broods. Mechanically I walk over to a tree, pull my cap low over my eyes and lean with my back against the tree, hands clasped behind my neck. I gaze and think, the flames from my fire dazzle my eyes, but I feel nothing. For some time I stand in this meaning-less attitude, looking into the fire. My legs are the first to forsake me, they grow weary, and I sit down stiffly. Only now do I think what I have been doing. Why did I stare so long into the fire?

Aesop lifts his head and listens; he hears foot-steps. Eva appears among the trees.

'I am depressed and full of sad thoughts to-night,' I say.

And in her sympathy she makes no answer.

'I love three things,' I say then. 'I love a dream of love I once had, I love you, and I love this patch of earth.'

'And which do you love best?'

'The dream.'

There is quiet again. Aesop knows Eva; he puts his head on one side and watches her. I murmur: 'I saw a girl on the path to-day; she was walking arm in arm with her lover. The girl pointed me out with her eyes and she could hardly keep from laughing as I went past.'

'What was she laughing at?'

'I don't know. I dare say at me. Why do you ask?'

'Did you know her?'

'Yes. I nodded to her.'

'And did she not know you?'

'No, she pretended not to know me. . . . But why do you sit there questioning me? It is hateful of you. You shall not get her name out of me.'

Pause.

I murmur again: 'What was she laughing at? She is a flirt; but what was she laughing at? In Christ's name, what have I done to her?'

Eva answers: 'It was hateful of her to laugh at you.'

'No, it was not hateful of her!' I shout. 'I won't have you sitting there abusing her. She never does anything hateful; and she was right to laugh at me. Be quiet, confound it, and leave me in peace, do you hear?'

And Eva, frightened, leaves me in peace. I look at her and at once regret my harsh words; I fall down before her and wring my hands.

'Go home, Eva. It is you I love best; how could I love a dream? It was just a joke, it is you I love. Go home now, I shall come to you to-morrow. Remember I am yours, yes, don't forget that. Good night.'

And Eva goes home.

THE third Iron Night, a night of supreme tension. If only there were some frost! Instead of frost there was a lingering heat after the sun of the day; the night was like a warm morass. I piled up the fire. . . .

'Eva, there are times when it is bliss to be dragged along by the hair. So distorted can the mind become. One can be dragged by the hair up hill and down dale; and if anybody asks what is happening, then one answers in ecstasy: I am being dragged along by the hair! And if they ask: But can't we help you, free you? then one replies: No. And if they ask: But can you bear it? then one replies: Yes, I can bear it, for I love the hand that drags me. . . . Do you know, Eva, what it is to hope?'

'Yes, I think so.'

'You know, Eva, hope is a strange thing, something quite uncanny. You might be walking along a path one morning hoping to meet someone you are fond of. And do you meet? No. Why not? Because that someone is busy that morning and is somewhere quite different. . . . I once knew an old blind Lapp up in the hills. For fifty-eight years he had not seen a thing, and now he was seventy. He imagined he was seeing better as time went on; things were improving steadily, he thought. If all went well, he would be able to make out the sun in a year or two. His hair was still black, but his eyes were quite white. When we sat smoking together in his turf hut, he talked about all the things he had seen before he went blind. He was tough and healthy, without feeling, imperishable, and he kept his hope. When it was time for me to go, he stepped out with me and began to point in various directions. That is the south, he said, and that the north; now you go first in that direction, and when you have gone a little distance down you turn off that way. Quite right! I answered. Then the Lapp gave a little contented laugh and said: You see, forty or fifty years ago I didn't know that, so I must be seeing better now than I used to. Things are getting steadily better. Then he bent down and crept into the turf hut again, that everlasting turf hut, his home on earth. And he sat as before in front of the fire, full of hope that in a few years he would be able to see the sun. . . . Eva, it is truly a strange thing, this hope. For instance, I am hoping now I shall forget the person I did not meet on the path this morning.'

'You speak so strangely.'

'It is the third of the Iron Nights. I promise you, Eva, I shall be a different man to-morrow. Let me be alone now. You will not know me again in the morning. I shall laugh and kiss you, my sweetest girl. Remember, I have but to-night, and then I am a different man, in just a few hours now. Good night, Eva.'

'Good night.'

I lie closer to the fire and watch the flames. A fir cone falls from its branch, and then a dry twig or two. The night is like a boundless deep. I close my eyes.

After an hour, all my senses are throbbing in rhythm, I am ringing with the great stillness, ringing with it. I look up at the crescent moon standing in the sky like a white shell and I feel a great love for it, I feel myself blushing. 'It is the moon,' I say softly and passionately, 'it is the moon!' And my heart beats gently towards it. Several minutes pass. A slight breeze springs up, an unnatural gust of wind strikes me, a strange rush of air. What is it? I look about me and see no one. The wind calls to me and my soul bows in obedience to the call, I feel myself lifted out of my context, pressed to an invisible breast, tears spring to my eyes, I tremble—God is standing somewhere near looking at me. Again some minutes pass. I turn my head, the strangely heavy air ebbs away and I see something like the back of a spirit who wanders soundlessly through the forest.

I struggle for a little while against a heavy stupor; with mind worn out by agitation and weary as death, I fall asleep.

When I woke the night was gone. Oh, for too long I had moped about, in a high fever, waiting to succumb to some sickness or other. Things had often seemed at cross purposes, I had seen everything with a jaundiced eye, a deep melancholy had possessed me.

Now that was all over.

## 27

IT is autumn. Summer is past, it vanished as quickly as it came. Ah, how quickly it went! The days are cold now, I hunt and fish and sing songs in the woods. And there are days when thick fog comes swirling in from the sea and envelops all in a mirky dimness. On such a day something happened. I lost my way and wandered far into the woods of the annex and came out at the Doctor's house. There were visitors there, the young ladies I had met before, dancing youth, capering foals.

A carriage came rolling up and stopped at the garden gate; Edvarda was sitting in the carriage. She started when she caught sight of me. 'Good-bye,' I said quietly. But the Doctor held me back. At first Edvarda was distressed by my presence, and looked down when I said anything; later she endured me better and even addressed a few short questions to me. She was strikingly pale, the mist lay grey and cold over her face. She did not leave the carriage.

'I have come on an errand,' she said, smiling. 'I have been to the parish church, but I didn't find any of you there; they said you were here. I have been driving about for hours trying to find you. We are having a little party to-morrow evening—the Baron is leaving next week—and I have been asked to invite you all. There will be dancing too. Until to-morrow evening, then.'

They all bowed and thanked her.

To me she added: 'Now please don't stay away, will you? Don't send some note at the last minute with excuses.' She did not say that to any of the others. Shortly afterwards she drove away.

I was so moved by this unexpected kindliness that I stole away from the company for a moment and was happy. Then I took my leave of the Doctor and his guests and set off for home. How gracious she was to me, how gracious! What can

I do for her in return? My hands grew numb,
I felt the cold run sweetly through my wrists. Oh
my God, I thought, here I am flapping about numb
with joy, I cannot clench my hands and in my
helplessness I am almost in tears. What is to be
done about it? . . . It was late in the evening when
I got home. I took the way past the quay and asked
a fisherman if the mail boat would be in by to-
morrow evening. Oh no, the mail boat would not
be in until some time next week. I hurried up to
the hut and began to examine my best suit. I brushed
it and cleaned it up; there were holes in it here and
there, and I wept as I mended the holes.

When I had finished, I lay down on the bed.
For a moment I am calm: a thought crosses my
mind and I leap up and stand stupefied in the
middle of the floor. 'The whole thing is again a
trick!' I whisper. I would not have been invited
if I had not chanced to be there when the others
were invited. Moreover, she had given me the
broadest hint to stay away—to send a note with
my excuses. . . .

I did not sleep at all that night; and when morning came, I went out into the forest, frozen, un-
rested and feverish. Ha, now they are preparing
for a party at Sirilund! What of it? I shall neither
go nor send any excuse. Herr Mack is a most
thoughtful man, he is giving this party for the
Baron; but I shall not appear at it, do you understand?

The mist lay thick over valley and hill, a clammy rime laid itself on my clothes and made them heavy, my face was cold and wet. Only now and then a breath of wind came, making the sleeping mists rise and fall, rise and fall.

The afternoon drew on, it was getting dark, the mist hid everything from my eyes, and I could not take my direction from the sun. I drifted about for hours on the way home, but nothing urged me to hurry; with the greatest calm I took wrong turnings and came upon unfamiliar places in the forest. At last I rested my gun against a tree and consulted my compass. I marked out my way carefully and began to walk. It may have been about eight or nine o'clock.

Then something happened.

After half an hour I hear music through the fog, and a few minutes later I recognise the place again; I am standing close beside the main building of Sirilund. Had my compass misdirected me to the very place I was trying to avoid? A familiar voice hails me—it is the Doctor's voice. Shortly after I am led in.

Oh, perhaps my gun barrel had deflected the compass so that it gave a wrong reading. The same thing has happened again to me since—one day this year. I do not know what to think. Perhaps it was fate.

## 28

ALL evening I had the bitter feeling I should not have gone to that party. My arrival went almost unnoticed, they were all much too taken up with one another; Edvarda barely bade me welcome. I began to drink heavily because I knew I was not welcome, and yet I did not leave.

Herr Mack smiled a lot and put on his most amiable expression; he was in evening dress and looked well. He flitted about the rooms, talked to his guests, dancing a dance now and then, laughing and joking. There were secrets lurking in his eyes.

A swirl of music and voices sounded through the whole house. Five of the rooms were crowded with guests, besides the big room where they were dancing. By the time I arrived they had had supper. Maids were now running about busily with glasses and wines, with coffee pots of burnished copper, with cigars and pipes and cakes and fruit. He had spared no expense. The chandeliers in the rooms had been provided with extra thick candles specially poured for the occasion; the new oil lamps were lit as well.

Eva was helping in the kitchen; I caught a glimpse of her. Strange that Eva was here as well!

The Baron was the centre of much attention, though he was quiet and modest and did not push himself forward. He too was in evening dress, the tails of which were sadly creased from having been packed. He talked a good deal with Edvarda, followed her about with his eyes, drank with her and addressed her as 'Fröken', as he did also the daughters of the Dean and the district surgeon. I felt a persistent dislike of him, and could hardly look at him without turning away again with a pained and stupid grimace. When he spoke to me I answered curtly and pressed my lips together after I had spoken.

I happen to recall one or two things from that evening. I stood talking to a young lady, a blonde girl, and I must have said something or told some story that made her laugh. I doubt if it was a very remarkable story, but perhaps I was tipsy and told it more amusingly than I remember now; at any rate I have forgotten what it was. In short, when I turned round, Edvarda was standing behind me. She gave me a look of approval.

Afterwards I noticed that she drew the blonde girl aside to hear what I had said. I cannot express how that look of Edvarda's cheered me after I had been going from room to room like an outcast all evening; at once I grew more light-hearted and afterwards I talked to a number of people and became quite sociable. As far as I know I was not guilty of any *faux-pas*. . . .

I was standing outside on the steps. Eva appeared from one of the rooms carrying some things. She saw me, came out on to the steps and hurriedly stroked my hand, whereupon she smiled and went in again. Neither of us had spoken. When I turned to go in after her, Edvarda was standing in the passage watching me. She looked straight at me. She did not speak either. I went into the ballroom.

' Just think, Lieutenant Glahn amuses himself by having *rendez-vous* with the servants outside on the steps! ' said Edvarda suddenly in a loud voice. She stood in the doorway. Several people heard what she said. She laughed as though she were joking, but her face was very pale.

I made no answer to this, I only murmured: ' It was quite by chance, she just came out and we met in the passage. . . .'

Time passed, an hour perhaps. One of the ladies had a glass spilt over her dress; as soon as Edvarda saw this, she cried: ' What's happening? Glahn has done that, of course.'

I had not done it, I was standing at the other end of the room when the accident occurred. After that, I drank pretty heavily again and kept near the door to be out of the way of the dancers.

The Baron continued to gather the ladies about himself, he regretted that his collections were already packed so that he could not show anything of them: the sample of sea-weed from the White

Sea, the clay from Korholmerne, the extraordinarily interesting rock formation from the sea bed. The ladies peeped curiously at his shirt studs, those five-pointed coronets that meant of course that he was a Baron. Under these circumstances the Doctor was having little success; even his witty oath ' Death and Torment ' no longer created any stir. But when Edvarda was speaking, he was always on the spot, correcting what she said, confusing her with his quibbles, keeping her down with calm superiority.

She said: ' . . . until I cross the valley of Death.'

' Cross what? ' the Doctor asked.

' The valley of Death. Isn't that what it's called, the valley of Death? '

' I have heard tell of the river of Death. That is surely what you mean.'

Later she talked about guarding something like a . . .

' Dragon,' the Doctor interrupted.

' That's right. Like a dragon,' she answered.

But the Doctor said: ' You can thank me for saving you there. I am certain you were going to say *Argus*.'

The Baron raised his eyebrows and looked at him in astonishment through his thick glasses. He had probably never heard such tomfoolery before. But the Doctor was quite unconcerned. What did he care about the Baron!

I continue to stand by the door. In the room

the dancing is going well. I manage to start a conversation with the governess from the vicarage. We talked about the war and the state of affairs in the Crimea, about the events in France, of Napoleon as Emperor and his protection of the Turk; the young lady had read the newspapers that summer and was able to tell me what the news was. Finally we sit down on a sofa and go on chatting.

Edvarda comes by and stops in front of us. Suddenly she says: 'The Lieutenant must forgive me for surprising him on the steps like that. I shall never do it again.'

And still she laughed, and did not look at me.

'You must stop this now, Miss Edvarda,' I said.

She had addressed me very formally; that meant no good, and her look was malicious. I thought of the Doctor, and shrugged my shoulders carelessly as he would have done. She said: 'But why does the Lieutenant not go out into the kitchen? Eva is there. I think that is where he ought to remain.'

And she gave me a look of hate.

I had not been to parties very often, but at the few I had attended I had never heard such a tone. I said: 'Are you not running the risk of being misunderstood, Miss Edvarda?'

'No. How? Yes, of course, it's possible, but how?'

'Sometimes you say things without thinking. Just now, for instance, it seemed to me as though you were actually turning me out into the kitchen, and that is of course a misunderstanding. After all, I know very well that it was not your intention to be rude.'

She walks a few steps away from us. I could see by her manner that she was thinking all the time about what I had said. She turns and comes back, she says breathlessly: 'That was no misunderstanding, Lieutenant; you heard quite correctly. I was turning you out into the kitchen.'

'Oh, but Edvarda!' the terrified governess exclaims.

And I began talking again about the War and the state of affairs in the Crimea; but my thoughts were far away from these things. I was no longer drunk, only completely confused; the ground slipped from under my feet and, as on so many unhappy occasions before, I was thrown off my balance. I get up from the sofa and want to go out. The Doctor stops me.

'I have this moment been listening to someone singing your praises,' he says.

'My praises? Who?'

'Edvarda. She is still standing over there in the corner, and looking at you with glowing eyes. I shall never forget it; from the look in her eyes you would say she was in love, and she said quite distinctly that she admired you.'

'That's good!' I said with a laugh. Oh, there was not a clear thought in my head.

I went over to the Baron, bent over him as though I wanted to whisper something, and when I was close enough I spat in his ear. He sprang up and looked at me, stupefied by what I had done. Afterwards I saw him telling Edvarda what had happened, and saw that it grieved her. No doubt she was thinking of the shoe I had flung into the water, of the cups and glasses I had been unfortunate enough to break, and all the other social blunders I had made; all that surely was resurrected in her mind again. I was ashamed, it was all over with me; whichever way I turned I met frightened and astonished looks. And I sneaked away from Sirilund without a word of leave-taking or thanks.

## 29

THE Baron is leaving; ah, well! I will load my gun and go up into the hills and fire a loud shot in his and Edvarda's honour. I will bore a deep hole in the cliff face and blow up a mountain in his and Edvarda's honour. And a great rock shall roll down the mountain and plunge mightily into the sea as his ship goes by. I know a spot, a cleft in the mountain where rocks have rolled before and made a clear path to the sea. Far below, there is a little jetty.

'Two drills,' I say to the smith.

And the smith whets two drills. . . .

Eva has been put to driving back and forth between the mill and the quay with one of Herr Mack's horses. She has to do a man's work transporting sacks of corn and flour. I meet her and she looks lovely with her fresh face. Dear God, how warm and tender is her smile! Every evening I met her.

'You look as if you hadn't a single care, Eva, my love.'

'You call me your love! I am an ignorant woman but I will be true to you. I will be true to you even if I have to die for it. Herr Mack gets harsher and harsher every day, but I don't think about it. He raves, but I don't answer him. He took hold of my arm and turned grey with fury. One thing does worry me.'

'And what is it that worries you?'

'Herr Mack is threatening you. He says to me: Ah, you have got your head full of that Lieutenant! And I answer: Yes, I belong to him. Then he says: Well, you wait, I'll soon get rid of him. He said that yesterday.'

'It means nothing, let him threaten. . . . Eva, let me see if your feet are as tiny as ever? Shut your eyes and let me see!'

And with her eyes shut she falls on my neck. Her body trembles. I carry her into the woods. The horse stands waiting.

## 30

I SIT up in the hills, drilling. The autumn air is crystal clear about me, the hammering on my drill rings out in a steady rhythm. Aesop looks at me with wondering eyes. A ripple of contentment runs occasionally through my breast; nobody knows that I am here on the bare fells.

The birds of passage have gone now—a pleasant journey and welcome back again! The titmouse and blackcap and an occasional hedge-sparrow now live alone on the screes and in the thickets: peep! peep! Everything is so strangely changed, the dwarf birch bleeds red against the grey stones; here a bluebell, there a hornet rising from the heather, swaying and humming a gentle song; hark! But away over everything flies the heron with neck outstretched, seeking its way into the mountains.

And evening comes; I put away my drill and my hammer under a stone to take a rest. Everything slumbers, the moon glides up in the north, the mountains cast gigantic shadows. The moon is full, it looks like a glowing island, a round mystery of brass that I stroll round and wonder at. Aesop is restless and gets up.

'What do you want, Aesop? As for me, I am weary of my sorrow, I want to forget it, drown it. I order you to lie still, Aesop, I don't want to be disturbed. Eva asks: Do you sometimes think of me? I answer: Always of you. Eva asks again: And does it give you joy to think of me? I answer: Sheer joy, never anything but joy. Then Eva says: Your hair is turning grey. I answer: Yes, it is starting to turn grey. But Eva asks: Is it turning grey because of something you are thinking about? And to this I answer: Perhaps. Finally Eva says: So you don't think only of me. . . . Lie still, Aesop, I'd rather tell you about something else instead. . . .'

But Aesop stands sniffing excitedly down in the direction of the valley, whining and tugging at my clothes. When at last I rise and follow, he cannot get along fast enough. A red glow shows in the sky above the trees, I push on faster, and there before my eyes appears a fire, an enormous bonfire. I stop and stare, walk a few steps and stare again— my hut is in flames.

# 31

THE fire was Herr Mack's work, I saw through it from the first moment. I lost my skins and my birds' wings, I lost my stuffed eagle; everything burnt. What now? For two nights I lay under the open sky without going to Sirilund to ask for shelter; at last I rented a deserted fishing hut near the quay, and plugged the cracks with dried moss. I slept on a cart-load of red heather from the hills. Once more I was installed.

Edvarda sent a message to say she had heard of my misfortune and now offered me on her father's behalf a room at Sirilund. Edvarda touched? Edvarda magnanimous? I sent no answer. I was, thank God, no longer without shelter, and felt a proud joy that I was able to ignore Edvarda's offer. I met her on the road with the Baron, they were walking arm in arm; I looked them both in the face and nodded as I passed. She stopped and asked: 'Won't you come and stay with us, Lieutenant?'

'I have already arranged my new place,' I said, stopping also.

She looked at me, her breast rose and fell.

' You wouldn't have come to any harm at our place,' she said.

Something like gratitude stirred in my heart, but I could not speak.

The Baron walked slowly on.

' Perhaps you never want to see me any more now,' she said.

' I must thank you, Miss Edvarda, for offering me shelter when my hut was burnt down,' I said. ' It was all the nobler of you since it can scarcely have been with your father's approval.' And I thanked her with bared head for her offer.

' In God's name, don't you ever want to see me again, Glahn?' she said suddenly.

The Baron called.

' The Baron is calling,' I said, and again removed my cap.

And I went up into the hills to my drilling. Nothing, nothing should make me lose my self-possession any more. I met Eva. ' There, you see!' I cried. ' Herr Mack cannot drive me away. He has burnt my hut down, and already I have another hut. . . .' She was carrying a brush and a tar bucket. ' What now, Eva?'

Herr Mack had careened a boat at the jetty under the cliff and had ordered her to tar it. He watched her every step, she had to obey.

' But why at the jetty, why not at the quay?'

Herr Mack had given instructions for it to be done that way. . . .

*143*

' Eva, Eva, my love, you are made a slave and you never complain. Look, now you are smiling again, and life surges in your smile although you are a slave.'

When I came to my mine, a surprise was waiting for me. I saw that somebody had been there; I examined the tracks in the rubble and recognised the imprint of Herr Mack's long, pointed shoes. What could he be ferreting about here for? I thought to myself and looked about. Nobody to be seen. No suspicion awoke in me.

And I began to hammer on my drill, never dreaming what madness I was doing.

# 32

THE mail boat came; it brought my uniform and it was to take the Baron and all his cases of shells and seaweed on board. Now it was loading barrels of herring and oil at the quay; towards evening it would sail again.

I take my gun and load both barrels with a quantity of powder. When I had done so, I nodded to myself. I go up into the hills and fill my drill-holes with powder as well; I nod again. Now everything was ready. I lay down to wait.

I waited for hours. All the time I could hear

the steamer's winches hoisting and lowering. It was already growing dusk. At last the whistle blows, the cargo is on board, the ship is leaving. Now I have a few minutes to wait. The moon was not up, and I stared like one insane through the gloom of the evening.

When the first point of the bow appeared round the islet I lit the fuse and withdrew hastily. A minute passes. Suddenly there is a roar, fragments of stone spurt up into the air, the hillside trembles and the rock rolls thundering down into the abyss. The hills all around give echo. I seize my gun and fire one barrel; the echo answers again and again and again. After a moment I fire the second barrel; the air quaked at my salute, and the echo flung the noise out into the wide world; it was as if all the hills had joined in a mighty shout for the departing vessel. A short time passes; the air grows still, the echo dies away among the hills, and the earth lies silent again. The ship disappears in the twilight.

I am still trembling with a strange excitement. I take my drills and my gun under my arm and set off down the hillside, my knees giving beneath me. I took the shortest way, keeping an eye on the smoking track left by my avalanche. Aesop goes shaking his head all the time and sneezes at the smell of scorching.

When I got down to the jetty, a sight awaited me that violently shocked my senses: a boat lay shattered by the falling rock, and Eva, Eva lay beside it, crushed and broken, smashed by the blow, torn beyond recognition down her side and below the waist. Eva was dead.

## 33

WHAT more is there for me to write? I fired no shot for many days; I had no food and I ate nothing; I sat in my shed. Eva was borne to the church in Herr Mack's white-painted houseboat, I walked overland and appeared at the graveside. . . .

Eva is dead. Do you remember her little girlish head with hair like a nun's? She came so quietly, laid down her burden and smiled. And did you see how life surged in that smile? Lie still, Aesop, I remember a strange tale from four generations ago, from the time of Iselin when Stamer was a priest.

A maid sat captive in a stone tower. She loved a lord. Why? Ask the wind and the stars, ask the God of Life; for none other knows these things. And the lord was her friend and her lover; but time passed and one fine day he saw another, and his feelings changed.

Like a youth he had loved his maid. Often he

called her his blessing and his dove; and her embrace was hot and throbbing. He said: 'Give me your heart!' And she did so. He said: 'May I ask something of you, my love?' And in ecstasy she answered: 'Yes.' She gave him all and he did not thank her.

This other he loved as a slave, as a mad man and as a beggar. Why? Ask the dust of the road and the leaves that fall, ask the mysterious God of Life; for none other knows these things. She gave him nothing; no, nothing did she give him and yet he thanked her. She said: 'Give me your peace and your reason.' And he grieved only that she did not ask his life.

And his maid was put in the tower. . . .

'What are you doing, maiden, you sit and smile?'

'I am thinking of something that is now ten years ago. It was then I met him.'

'You remember him still?'

'I remember him still.'

And time passes. . . .

'What are you doing, maiden? And why do you sit and smile?'

'I am sewing his name on a cloth.'

'Whose name? Of him who shut you away?'

'Yes, of him I met twenty years ago.'

'You remember him still?'

'I remember him as before.'

And time passes. . . .

'What are you doing, prisoner?'

'I grow old and can no longer see to sew, I scrape the plaster from the walls. From the plaster I shall make a jar for him, as a little gift for him.'

'Of whom are you speaking?'

'Of my lover, of him who shut me away in the tower.'

'You smile because he shut you away?'

'I am thinking of what he will say now. See, see! he will say, my maid has sent me a little jar, she has not forgotten me these thirty years.'

And time passes. . . .

'What, prisoner, you sit doing nothing and you smile?'

'I am growing old, I am growing old, my eyes are blind, I only think.'

'Of him you met forty years ago?'

'Of him I met when I was young. Perhaps it is forty years ago.'

'But do you not know then that he is dead? Old woman, you blench, you do not answer, your lips are white, you breathe no more. . . .'

See, thus it was with the strange tale of the maid in the tower. Stay, Aesop, I forgot something. One day she heard her lover's voice in the court-yard, and she fell on her knees and blushed. She was then forty years old. . . .

I bury you, Eva, and in humility kiss the sand on your grave. A rich, rose-red memory passes through my heart when I think of you; felicity floods over me when I remember your smile. You gave all, all did you give; and it cost you no painful surrender, for you were the wild child of life itself. Yet others, who grudgingly husband even their glances, seem to have all my thoughts. Why? Ask the twelve months and the ships at sea, ask the mysterious God of the heart. . . .

## 34

A MAN said: 'Have you given up shooting now? Aesop has scented something in the woods, he is chasing a hare.'

I said: 'Go and shoot it for me.'

Some days passed. Herr Mack called on me: he was hollow-eyed, his face was grey. I thought: is it true I can see through my fellow men, or is it not? I myself do not know.

Herr Mack spoke of the landslide, the catastrophe. It was an accident, a distressing coincidence, I was in no way to blame.

I said: 'If there was someone who wanted to separate Eva and me at any price, he has succeeded. God damn him!'

Herr Mack eyed me suspiciously. He murmured something about the lovely funeral. No expense had been spared.

I sat and marvelled at his ready evasiveness.

He did not want any compensation for the boat my landslide had smashed.

'Oh, but surely!' I said. 'Will you really not take any payment for the boat, and for the tar bucket and brush?'

'My dear Lieutenant!' he answered. 'How can you think such a thing!'

And he looked at me with hate in his eyes.

FOR three weeks I saw nothing of Edvarda. Oh, yes; once I ran into her at the store where I had gone to buy bread; she stood behind the counter and was rummaging through various pieces of material. Apart from her, only the two assistants were there.

I greeted her, and she looked up but did not answer. Then it occurred to me that I did not want to ask for bread while she was there; I turned to the assistants and asked for powder and shot. While these were being weighed I kept my eye on her.

A grey dress, much too small for her, its button-holes worn; her flat breast heaved desperately. How she had grown during the summer! Her brow was pensive, those strange arched eyebrows were set in her face like two riddles, all her movements had become more mature. I looked at her hands, the expression in her long, delicate fingers affected me powerfully and made me tremble. She was still turning over the materials.

I stood wishing that Aesop would run to her behind the counter and recognise her; then I could call him back at once and apologise. What would she answer then?

' Here you are,' said the assistant.

I paid, took my parcels and again murmured my respects. She looked up, but again did not answer. Good, I thought. She is quite likely already betrothed to the Baron. And I left without bread.

When I was outside, I glanced up at the window. No one was looking out for me.

## 35

THEN one night the snow came and it began to be chilly in my hut. There was a fireplace where I cooked my food, but the wood burned badly and many draughts came through the walls, although I had plugged them as well as I could. Autumn was over and the days grew short. The first snow still melted in the sun and again the ground lay bare; but the nights were cold, and the water froze. And all the grass and all the insects died.

A mysterious stillness came over the people, they brooded in silence, their eyes waited for the winter. No longer did shouts come across from the drying grounds; the harbour lay quiet, everything was making ready for the endless night of the northern lights when the sun slept in the sea. Dully, dully came the sound of oars from a solitary boat.

A girl came rowing.

' Where have you been, my child? '

' Nowhere.'

' Nowhere? Wait, I know you, I met you in the summer.'

She brought the boat in, stepped ashore and made fast.

' You were herding goats, you were knitting a stocking, I met you one night.'

A faint blush rises to her cheeks and she laughs shyly.

' My little wanton! Come into the hut and let me look at you. I know your name too, it is Henriette.'

But she walks past me in silence. The autumn, the winter has laid hold of her; already her senses were aslumber.

Already the sun had gone into the sea.

## 36

AND for the first time I put on my uniform and went down to Sirilund. My heart was beating.

I remembered everything of that first day when Edvarda rushed over to me and embraced me in the sight of everybody; now for many months she had cast me up and cast me down and my hair had turned grey over it. My own fault? Yes, my stars had led me astray. I thought: How it will gratify her if I throw myself at her feet to-day and tell her the secret of my heart! She will offer me a chair and call for some wine and, as she raises the glass to her lips to drink with me, she will say: ' Thank you, Lieutenant, for the times we have had together, I shall never forget them! ' But if I then am pleased and harbour a little hope, she will only pretend to drink and set down the glass untouched. And she will not hide from me the fact that she only pretended to drink, she will make it quite obvious. She is like that.

Good, the final hour will soon be striking!

And as I walked down the road, I thought: My uniform will impress her, the braid is new and elegant. The sabre will rattle on the floor. I trembled with nervous pleasure and I whispered to myself: Who knows what may happen yet! I raised my head and made a gesture with my hand. No more humility now, but honour and pride! It was all the same to me whatever the outcome, I would make no further advances. Forgive me, fair damosel, that I do not court you. . . .

Herr Mack met me outside in the courtyard, greyer and still more hollow-eyed.

' Leaving? Ah, yes, of course. You haven't been too comfortable lately, eh? Your hut was burnt down.' And Herr Mack smiled.

Suddenly it was as if I saw before me the cleverest man in the world.

' Go in, Lieutenant, Edvarda is at home. Well, good-bye. I dare say we'll see each other at the quay when the boat sails.' He walked away with bowed head, thinking, whistling.

Edvarda was sitting in the drawing-room, reading. She was startled for a moment as I entered in my uniform; she looked sideways at me like a bird and even blushed. She opened her mouth.

' I have come to say good-bye,' I managed to get out at last.

At once she rose and I saw that my words had had an effect on her.

' Glahn, are you going away? Now? '

' As soon as the ship comes.' I seize her hand, both her hands, a senseless rapture takes possession of me and I burst out: ' Edvarda! ' and stare at her.

And in an instant she is cold, cold and defiant. Everything in her resisted me, she drew herself up. I found myself standing like a beggar before her, I dropped her hands and let her go. For the next moment or two I remember I stood there repeating mechanically: 'Edvarda! Edvarda!' again and again without thinking; and when she asked: 'Yes? What were you going to say?' I told her nothing.

'To think that you are leaving already!' she said again. 'Who will come next year, I wonder?'

'Another,' I answered. 'The hut will be rebuilt, no doubt.'

Pause. She was already reaching for her book.

'I regret my father is not at home,' she said. 'But I shall tell him you were here.'

To this I made no reply. I stepped forward, took her hand once more and said: 'Good-bye, Edvarda.'

'Good-bye!' she answered.

I opened the door as if to go. Already she was sitting with the book in her hand, reading, really reading and turning the pages. My leaving had made no impression on her, absolutely none.

I coughed.

She turned and said in surprise: 'Oh, haven't you gone? I thought you had gone.'

God alone knows, but her surprise was too great, she was not careful enough and exaggerated her astonishment; and I had the impression that she had perhaps known all the time I was standing behind her.

'Now I am going,' I said.

Then she rose and came over to me.

'I should like something to remind me of you when you have gone,' she said. 'There was something I thought of asking you for, but perhaps it is too much. Will you give me Aesop?'

Without reflecting I answered 'Yes'.

'Then perhaps you would come and bring him to-morrow,' she said.

I went.

I looked up at the window. Nobody there.

It was all over now. . . .

T HE last night in the hut. I brooded, I counted the hours; when morning came I prepared my last meal. It was a cold day.

Why had she asked me to come and bring the dog myself? Did she want to talk to me, tell me something for the last time? I had nothing more to hope for. And how would she treat Aesop? Aesop, Aesop, she will torment you! Because of me she will whip you, caress you too perhaps, but certainly whip you in and out of season and utterly destroy you. . . .

I called Aesop, patted him, put our two heads together and reached for my gun. He was already whining with pleasure, thinking we were going out hunting. Again I put our heads together, placed the muzzle of the gun against Aesop's neck and fired.

I hired a man to carry Aesop's body to Edvarda.

## 37

THE mail boat was to sail later that afternoon. I took myself down to the quay, my things were already on board. Herr Mack shook me by the hand and said encouragingly I would have nice weather, pleasant weather, he would not mind a trip himself in such weather. The Doctor came walking down, Edvarda was with him; I felt my knees beginning to tremble.

'We wanted to see you safely on board,' said the Doctor.

I thanked him.

Edvarda looked me straight in the face and said: 'I must express my thanks to the Lieutenant for his dog.' She pressed her lips together, they were white. Again she had addressed me with exaggerated formality.

'When does the boat go?' the Doctor asked a man.

'In half an hour.'

I said nothing.

Edvarda turned agitatedly this way and that.

'Doctor, shall we not go home again now?' she said. 'I have done what was my errand.'

'You have completed your errand,' said the Doctor.

She laughed with humiliation at his eternal corrections and replied: 'Wasn't that more or less what I said?'

'No,' he answered curtly.

I looked at him. The little man stood there cold and firm; he had made a plan and was following it to the bitter end. And what if in spite of all he lost? Whatever the outcome, he would never show it: his face never betrayed him.

It was growing dark.

'Well, good-bye!' I said. 'And thank you for every single day.'

Edvarda looked at me dumbly. Then she turned her head and stood looking out at the ship.

I climbed into the boat. Edvarda was still standing on the quay. When I was standing on board, the Doctor shouted good-bye. I looked over to the shore; that same moment Edvarda turned for home and walked away from the quay, hurriedly, with the Doctor far behind her. That was the last I saw of her.

A wave of sadness passed through my heart. . . .

The steamer began to move; I could still make out Herr Mack's signboard: *Salt and Barrel Depot.* But it soon grew indistinct. The moon and the stars came out, the mountains rose up round about and I saw the endless forests. There is the mill; there, there lay the hut that was burnt down; the big grey boulder stands there in solitude on the site of the fire. Iselin, Eva. . . .

The night of the Northern lights spreads over valley and hill.

# *38*

I HAVE written this to while away the time. It amused me to think back to that summer in Nordland when often I counted the hours and yet time flew. All is changed; the days will no longer pass.

I still have many a gay moment; but time, time stands still and I cannot understand how it can stand so still. I have left the service now and am free as a prince, all is well, I meet people, drive in carriages; now and then I close one eye and write with my forefinger on the sky; I tickle the moon under the chin and I fancy I see it laugh, convulsed with foolish laughter at being tickled under the chin. All things smile. I set the corks popping and call in gay people.

As for Edvarda, I do not think about her. Why should I not have completely forgotten her after all this time? I am a man of pride and honour. And if anybody asks me if I have any worries, then straight off I answer: No, I have no worries.

Cora lies looking at me. At one time it was Aesop, but now it is Cora that lies looking at me. The clock ticks over the fireplace; outside my open windows is the busy roar of the city. There is a knock at the door and the postman hands me a letter. A letter with a coronet. I know who it is from, I understand it at once or perhaps I dreamt it one sleepless night. But there is no message in the letter; it holds only two green bird's feathers.

An icy terror runs through me, I grow cold. Two green feathers! I say to myself. Well, what is to be done about it? But why should I grow cold? What a damned draught there is now from those windows.

And I shut the windows.

There lie two bird's feathers, I think to myself again; I feel somehow I ought to know them, they remind me of a little joke up in Nordland, just one little incident among many other incidents; it was amusing to see those two feathers again. And suddenly I see a face and hear a voice and the voice says: ' There you are, Lieutenant, there are your bird's feathers! '

Your bird's feathers. . . .

' You must lie still, Cora, do you hear! I will beat the life out of you if you move! '

The weather is hot, unbearably hot; what was I thinking of when I shut the windows! Open wide the windows, throw open the door, this way, you merry people, come in!  Hey, messenger, I want you to go and fetch a lot of people. . . .

And the day passes, but time stands still.

I HAVE written this now just for my own pleasure and amused myself as best I could. No worries weigh on me, I merely long to go away, I know not where, but far away, perhaps to Africa or to India; for I belong to the forests and the solitude.

# GLAHN'S DEATH

*A paper from the year* 1861

# I

THE Glahn family may advertise in the papers as long as they like for news of the missing Lieutenant Thomas Glahn; but he will never come back again. He is dead, and I even know how he died.

To tell the truth, I am not surprised that his family should go on making enquiries; for Thomas Glahn was in many ways an unusual and likeable man. In justice to him I must admit this, in spite of the fact that in my soul I still feel hostility towards Glahn and the memory of him rouses my hatred. He looked magnificent, was full of youthful vigour and had an irresistible way with him. When he looked at you with his animal eyes, you could not help feeling his power; even I felt it. A woman is supposed to have said: ' When he looks at me I am lost; I feel as though he were touching me.'

But Thomas Glahn had his faults, and I am not disposed to conceal them, since I hate him. At times he could be full of nonsense like a child, so good-natured was he, and perhaps it was this that so bewitched the women, God knows! He could gossip with them and laugh at their senseless twaddle, and by this he made his impression on them. Once he said about a very corpulent man in the town that he looked as if he was walking about with his trousers full of lard, and he laughed at this joke himself, although I would have been ashamed of it. Another time, after we had come to live in the same house together, he showed his silliness in a most obvious way; my landlady came in one morning and asked what I wanted for breakfast, and in my hurry I happened to answer: ' A bread and a slice of egg.' Thomas Glahn was sitting in my room at the time—he was living in the attic room above, close under the roof—and he began to laugh as any child might at this little slip of the tongue, delighted with it. ' A bread and a slice of egg,' he kept on saying over and over again, until I looked at him in astonishment and caused him to be silent.

Perhaps I shall remember some other of his ridiculous traits later on, and if so I shall set them down as well; I will not spare him, for he is still an enemy of mine. Why should I be magnanimous? But I will admit that he talked nonsense only when he was drunk. But is not being drunk a big fault in itself?

When I met him in the autumn of 1859, he was a man of thirty-two—we were about the same age. At that time he had a full beard and wore woollen hunting shirts with excessively low-cut necks, and it happened also that he not infrequently left the top button undone. At first, his neck struck me as being remarkably handsome; but little by little he made me his deadly enemy, and then I did not think his neck any finer than mine, even though I did not show it off as much. The first time I met him was on a river boat; I was making for the same place as he was on a hunting trip, and we agreed at once to go up country together by ox-cart when the railway could take us no further. I am deliberately avoiding any mention of the place we went to, for I do not want to put anybody on the track; but the Glahn family can safely stop advertising for news of their relative; for he lies dead at that place we went to, which I do not wish to name.

I had moreover heard tell of Thomas Glahn before I met him; his name was not unfamiliar to me. I had heard that he had been involved with a young girl in Nordland, from one of the big houses, and that he had compromised her in some way or another, whereupon she had broken with him. For this he had sworn in foolish spite to take revenge upon himself; and the lady, quite unperturbed, let him do as he pleased, it was no concern of hers. Only from then on did Thomas Glahn's name become really well known; he ran wild, behaved like mad, he drank, created scandal after scandal, and resigned his commission. That was a queer way of taking revenge for a jilting!

There was also another story going the rounds about his relations with that young lady: that he had not compromised her at all, but that her family had thrown him out of the house and that she herself had not objected, for a Swedish Count, whose name I do not want to mention, had started to pay court to her. But this report I am less inclined to believe; I consider the first one more likely, for after all I hate Thomas Glahn and I am ready to believe the worst of him. But however it was, he himself never spoke about this affair with the distinguished lady, nor did I ask him about it. What concern was it of mine?

As we sat there on the river boat, I cannot remember talking about anything else but the little village we were making for, to which neither of us had been before.

'I am told there is a sort of hotel there,' said Glahn, looking at the map. 'If we are lucky, we might be able to stay there; they say it is kept by an old English half-breed woman. The chieftain lives in. the next village and is supposed to have many wives, some of them only ten years old.'

Well, I had no idea whether or not the chieftain had many wives or whether there was an hotel in the place, so I said nothing; but Glahn smiled and I thought his smile was very attractive.

I forgot to mention, by the way, that he could not by any means be called a perfect man, even though he looked so handsome. He told me himself he had an old gunshot wound in his left foot and that he suffered much from arthritis whenever the weather changed.

## 2

A WEEK later we were installed in the big hut that passed for an hotel, with the old English half-breed woman. Oh, what an hotel! The walls were of mud and some wood, and the wood was eaten away by the white ants that crawled about everywhere. I lived in a room off the sitting-room, with a green glass window looking on to the street, a single pane which was not very clear; and Glahn had chosen a tiny hole up in the attic, where he also had a window on to the street, but where it was much darker and much more miserable to live. The sun beat on the thatched roof and made his room almost unbearably hot day and night; moreover there was no staircase up to his place but only a miserable ladder with four rungs. Was it my fault? I gave Glahn the choice and said: ' There are two rooms here, one upstairs and one down, take your pick! '

And Glahn looked at the two rooms and took the upper one, perhaps to give me the best one—but did I perhaps not show my gratitude to him for it? I owe him nothing.

So long as the worst of the heat lasted we gave hunting a miss and stayed quietly at the hut, for

the heat was terribly bad. We lay at night with a
mosquito net round the bed because of the insects;
but even then it sometimes happened that blind
bats would come hurtling silently against the nets
and tear them; this happened very often to Glahn
because he had to keep a trap open in the roof on
account of the heat, but it did not happen to me.
During the day we lay on mats outside the hut
and smoked and observed the life of the other huts.
The natives were a brown and thick-lipped people,
all with rings in their ears and dead, brown eyes;
they were almost naked with just a strip of cotton
cloth or plaited leaves round their loins, and the
women had also a short cotton skirt to cover them.
All the children were stark naked day and night,
with great protruding bellies that glistened with oil.

' The women are too fat,' said Glahn.

And I thought the women were too fat as well;
and perhaps it was not Glahn after all, but I, who
thought that first; but I shall not dispute his claim
and readily give him the credit. As a matter of
fact not all the women were ugly, though their faces
were fat and swollen; I had met a girl in the village,
a young half-Tamil girl with long hair and snow-
white teeth, she was the prettiest of them all. I
came upon her one evening on the edge of a paddy-
field, she was lying face down in the long grass
kicking her legs in the air. She could talk to me,
and we talked to each other as long as I wanted;
it was nearly morning before we parted, and then

she did not take the straight way home but pretended she had spent the night in the next village. Glahn was sitting that evening outside a little hut in the middle of our village with two other girls who were very young, perhaps themselves not more than ten years old. There he sat fooling with them and drinking rice beer with them; that was the sort of thing he liked.

A few days later we went out hunting. We passed tea plantations, paddy-fields and grassy plains; we left the village behind us and followed the line of the river, through forests of strange foreign trees, bamboo and mango, tamarind, teak and salt-trees, oil and rubber plants, and God knows what other sorts of trees as well; we neither of us understood very much about it. But there was little water in the river, and so it would remain until the rainy season. We shot wild pigeons and wildfowl, and saw a couple of panthers late one afternoon; parrots too flew over our heads. Glahn shot with deadly accuracy, he never missed, but that was because his gun was better than mine; many a time I shot with deadly accuracy as well. I never boasted about it, but Glahn would often say: ' I'll sting that one in the tail ' or ' I'll scratch that one's head for him.' He would say this before he fired; and when the bird dropped, sure enough he had hit it in the tail or the head as he had said. When we ran across the two panthers, Glahn was all for attacking them too with his shotgun, but

I persuaded him to give up the idea as it had begun to grow dark and we had no more than a couple of cartridges left. He made quite a song about that too, about being brave enough to want to attack panthers with a shotgun.

'I am annoyed that I didn't fire after all,' he said to me. 'What do you want to be so damned cautious for? Do you want to live long?'

'I am glad you consider me wiser than yourself,' I answered.

'Well, let's not fall out over a little thing like that,' he said.

Those were his words, not mine; if he had wanted to fall out with me, I would not have minded. I was beginning to dislike him for his frivolous behaviour and his ways with the women. Only the night before I had been walking quietly along with my little friend Maggie, the Tamil girl, and we were both in the best of spirits. Glahn is sitting there outside the hut, and he nods and smiles to us as we walk past; but Maggie saw him then for the first time and asked me all sorts of questions about him. So great was the impression he had made on her that when it was time to go we went our separate ways: she did not come home with me.

Glahn wanted to make light of it when I spoke to him about it, as if it were something of no importance. But I did not forget it. Nor had it been to me he had nodded and smiled as we passed by the hut; it was to Maggie.

' What's that she is always chewing? ' he asked
me.

' I don't know,' I answered. ' She just chews, I
suppose, that's what she's got teeth for.'

It was not new to me that Maggie was always
chewing something, I had noticed that long before.
But it was not betel she chewed, for her teeth were
quite white; however she had the habit of chewing
all sorts of other things, putting them in her mouth
to chew as though they were something nice. Anything would do: coins, bits of paper, feathers, she
chewed them all. Still, it was nothing to reproach
her for when she was, in spite of it all, the prettiest
girl in the village; but Glahn was envious of me,
that was it.

As a matter of fact, the next evening I was
friends again with Maggie, and we saw nothing of
Glahn.

## 3

A WEEK passed now; we went out shooting
daily and shot plenty of game. One morning just as we were entering the forest Glahn
gripped my arm and whispered: ' Stop! ' At the
same instant he threw up his rifle and fired. It
was a young leopard he had shot. I could quite
easily have shot it myself, but Glahn kept the

honour for himself and shot first. How he will brag about that now, I thought. We approached the dead animal; it was stone dead, ripped open along the left flank and with the bullet in its back.

Now I am not fond of having my arm gripped, so I said: 'I could also have managed that shot myself.'

Glahn looked at me.

I went on: 'Perhaps you don't think I could have done it?'

Still Glahn does not answer. Instead he once more shows his childishness and shoots the dead leopard again, this time through the head. I look at him astounded.

'Well,' he went on to explain, 'I can't have people saying I hit a leopard in the flank.'

It was too much for his vanity to have made such a poor shot; he always had to be first. What a fool he was! But this business was nothing to do with me, I would not give him away.

When we arrived back at the village in the evening with the dead leopard, a lot of the natives came out to look at it. But Glahn simply said we had shot it in the morning, and made no more of it than that. Maggie also came up and joined us.

'Who shot it?' she asked.

And Glahn answered: 'You can see for yourself, two bullet holes; we shot it this morning when we went out.' And he turned the beast over and showed her the two bullet holes, one in the flank and one in the head. 'That's where my bullet went,' he said, pointing to the one in the flank; in his frivolous way he wanted to let me take the credit for having shot it in the head. I could not be bothered to correct him, so I said nothing. After that, Glahn began treating the natives to rice beer, offering any amount of it to any who cared to drink.

'You both shot it,' said Maggie to herself, but she looked all the time at Glahn.

I drew her to one side and said: 'Why do you look the whole time at him? Am I not standing here close by as well ?'

'Yes,' she said. 'And listen: I am coming this evening.'

The next day Glahn got that letter. A letter came for him by express messenger from the river station, and it had gone a roundabout way of a hundred and eighty miles. The letter was written in a woman's hand and I thought it was probably from that former friend of his, the distinguished lady. Glahn laughed nervously when he had read it and gave the messenger something extra for bringing it. But it was not long before he became gloomy and silent and did nothing but sit and stare straight in front of him. That evening he got drunk in the company of an old dwarf of a native and his son; and he embraced me too and insisted on my having a drink.

'You are very genial to-night,' I said.

Then he laughed very loudly and said: ' Here we are now, the two of us, stuck in the middle of India shooting game, eh? Isn't that horribly funny? Here's to all the lands and realms of the world, and here's to all pretty women, married and unmarried, near and far. Ha! ha! Imagine a man, and a married woman making advances to him, a married woman!'

' A countess,' I said spitefully. I said it very spitefully and that hurt him. He whined like a dog because it hurt him. Then suddenly he wrinkled his forehead and began blinking his eyes and wondering if he had said too much, so solemnly did he take his precious secret. But just at that moment a number of children came running over to our hut, shouting and screaming: ' Tigers, ohoi, tigers!' A child had been pounced on by a tiger quite close to the village, in a thicket between the village and the river.

That was enough for Glahn, who was drunk and distracted in his mind; he seized his rifle and raced off at once to the thicket; he did not even have a hat on. But why did he take his rifle instead of his shotgun if he really was so brave? He had to wade across the river, and that was not without danger, but then the river was practically dry now until the rainy season; a moment later I heard two shots, followed directly by a third. Three shots for one animal! A lion would only have needed two, and this was merely a tiger! But even these three shots were no use, the child was mangled and half eaten by the time Glahn arrived on the spot; if he had not been so drunk he would not even have made the attempt to save it.

He spent the night drinking and carrying on in the hut next door, with a widow and her two daughters—God knows which of them he was with.

For two days Glahn was never sober a single minute; and he had also persuaded several others to drink with him. In vain he invited me to take part in the orgy; he did not care any longer what he said, and taunted me with being jealous of him.

'Your jealousy makes you blind,' he said.

My jealousy! I jealous of him!

'Listen to him!' I said. 'I jealous of you! What should I be jealous of you for?'

'All right, then! So you are not jealous of me,' he answered. 'By the way, I saw Maggie this evening. She was chewing as usual.'

I bit back my reply and went.

## 4

WE began to go out hunting again. Glahn felt he had wronged me and asked my forgiveness.

'I'm dead sick of everything, anyway,' he said. 'I only wish you would miss your aim one day and put a bullet in my throat.' Maybe it was that letter from the Countess again smouldering in his memory. I answered: 'As a man sows, so shall he reap.'

Day by day he grew more silent and morose; he had stopped drinking and went about without saying a word; his cheeks became hollow.

Suddenly one day I heard talking and laughter outside my window; I looked out. Glahn had a cheerful look again, he stood there talking in a loud voice to Maggie. He was using all his tricks to try to charm her. Maggie must have come straight from home, and Glahn had been watching for her. They had not even hesitated to associate right outside my window.

I felt a trembling in all my limbs, I cocked my rifle, but then I uncocked it again. I went on to the street and took Maggie by the arm; we walked out of the village in silence; Glahn at once disappeared into the hut.

'Why were you talking to him again?' I asked Maggie.

She did not reply.

I was sick with despair, my heart was beating so hard I could scarcely breathe. I had never seen Maggie looking lovelier; I had never even seen a white girl so lovely and therefore I forgot that she was a Tamil, forgot everything because of her.

'Answer me!' I said. 'Why do you talk to him?'

'I like him best,' she said.

'You like him better than me?'

'Yes.'

So! She liked him better than me, though I was as good a man as he was any day! Had I not always been kind to her and given her money and presents? And what had he done?

'He makes fun of you, he says you are always chewing,' I said.

She did not understand; and I explained to her that she had a habit of putting all sorts of things in her mouth and chewing them, and Glahn laughed at her for it. That made a deeper impression on her than anything else I had said.

'Look, Maggie,' I went on, 'I want you to be mine for always, wouldn't you like that? I've been thinking it over, you must come with me when I leave here. Listen, we'll get married and we'll go to my own country and live there. You would like that, wouldn't you?'

And that also impressed her. Maggie became lively and talked to me a lot on our walk. Only once did she mention Glahn; she asked: ' And will Glahn go with us when we go away? '

' No,' I said, ' he won't. Are you sorry about that? '

' No, no,' she replied quickly. ' I am glad about it.'

She said no more about him and I felt easier. And Maggie also came home with me when I asked her to.

When she left me a few hours later I climbed up the ladder to Glahn's room and knocked at the thin reed door. He was in. I said: ' I came to tell you that perhaps we had better not go out hunting to-morrow.'

' Why not? ' Glahn asked.

' Because I can't guarantee I won't miss my aim and put a bullet through your throat.'

Glahn did not answer and I went down again. After a warning like that he surely would not dare go out hunting to-morrow. But then why had he wanted to get Maggie over beneath my window and carry on with her there at the top of his voice? Why did he not go back home again if that letter really called him back? Instead of which he kept going about clenching his teeth and shouting to the winds: ' Nevermore! Nevermore! I'll be drawn and quartered first! '

But the morning after I had given Glahn this

warning, there he stood just the same beside my bed, shouting: 'Up, up, my friend! It's a lovely day, we must shoot something. And what you said last night, that was all nonsense.'

It was no more than four o'clock, but I got up at once and made ready to go off with him, because he had disdained my warning. I loaded my gun before setting out and let him stand and watch me doing it. It was, moreover, not a lovely day at all as he had said; it was raining, and this was just another one of his ways of mocking me. But I took no notice and went along with him in silence.

All that day we ranged through the forest, each with his own thoughts. We shot nothing, we missed one chance after another because we were thinking of other things than the chase. About mid-day Glahn began walking a little ahead of me, as if he wanted to give me a better opportunity of doing to him what was in my mind. He walked right in front of the muzzle of my gun, a piece of studied effrontery that I also ignored. That evening we returned home without anything having happened. I thought to myself: 'Perhaps he'll be more careful now and leave Maggie in peace.'

'This has been the longest day of my life,' Glahn said that evening as we stood by the hut.

Nothing more passed between us.

For the next few days he was in the blackest of moods, presumably all because of that same letter. 'I can't bear it! No, I can't bear it!' he would sometimes call out in the night; we could hear it all through the hut. His ill-temper was such that he refused to answer even the friendliest of questions when our landlady spoke to him; and he used to moan in his sleep. He must have a lot on his conscience, I thought, but why in the world does he not go home? His pride forbade him, I expect; he did not want to be the sort who comes crawling back after once having been rebuffed.

I met Maggie every evening, and Glahn no longer spoke to her. I noticed that she had given up chewing, she never chewed now, and I was pleased about that, and thought: Now she doesn't chew any more and that is one defect less, and now I love her twice as much! One day she asked after Glahn, asked very cautiously. Was he not well? Had he gone away?

'If he isn't dead or hasn't gone away,' I said, 'then I suppose he is lying there at home. It's all the same to me. He is absolutely unbearable now.'

But just as we arrived at the hut, we caught sight of Glahn lying on a mat on the ground, his hands clasped behind his neck, staring up at the sky.

'There he is, anyway,' I said.

Maggie went straight over to him before I could stop her and said in a happy sort of voice: 'I don't chew any more now, see for yourself; no chewing feathers or money or bits of paper any more.'

Glahn scarcely looked at her and went on quietly lying there; Maggie and I walked on. When I reproached her for having broken her promise by speaking to Glahn, she answered she had only meant to rebuke him.

'That's right, rebuke him,' I said. 'But was it for his sake you stopped chewing?'

She did not answer. What, would she not answer?

'Do you hear? You must tell me, was it for his sake?'

'No, no,' she said then, 'it was for your sake.'

And I really could not see why it should þe otherwise. Why should she do anything for Glahn's sake?

That evening Maggie promised to come to me; and she came.

## ſ

SHE came at ten o'clock, I heard her voice outside; she was talking in a loud voice to a child she led by the hand. Why did she not come in, and why had she the child with her? I watch her, and I begin to suspect that in talking so loud to the child she is giving a sort of signal; I also notice that she keeps her eyes fixed on the attic, on Glahn's window. Had he nodded to her, perhaps, or waved to her from inside when he heard her talking there? Anyhow, I had enough sense to know that one does not need to look up at the sky when one is speaking to a child on the ground.

I was on the point of going out to her and taking her by the arm; but just then she let go of the child's hand, she left the child standing there and came in herself through the door of the hut. She stepped into the passage. Well, there she was at last; I would have to scold her severely when she came!

There I stand and I can hear Maggie's step in the passage; there is no mistake, she is just outside my door. But then I hear her steps on the ladder, going up to the attic, to Glahn's hovel, instead of coming in to me; I hear it only too well. I push my door wide open but Maggie has already arrived upstairs, the door shuts behind her and I hear nothing more. That was at ten o'clock.

I go into my own room again and sit down; I take my gun and load it although it is the middle of the night. At twelve o'clock I go up the ladder and listen at Glahn's door. I can hear Maggie inside, can hear that she is being kind to Glahn, and I go down again. At one o'clock I go up again; all is quiet. I wait outside the door till they wake. Three o'clock, four o'clock; at five they woke. Good, I thought to myself; and I could think of nothing but that they were awake now, and that that was good. But shortly after I heard noises and movement down in my landlady's room, and I had to scurry down again quickly so as not to let her surprise me there. Glahn and Maggie were obviously awake and I could have overheard a great deal more, but I had to go.

In the passage I said to myself: ' See, here she went, brushing my door with her arm, but she did not open the door; she went up the ladder, and here is the ladder; these are the four steps she trod.'

My bed had not been slept in, nor did I lie down now; I sat by the window, fingering my rifle. My heart did not beat, it quaked.

Half an hour later I hear Maggie's footstep again on the ladder. I lie close to the window and I see her walk out of the hut. She was wearing her little cotton skirt that did not even reach to her knees, and over her shoulders a woollen scarf she had borrowed from Glahn. Apart from that she was quite naked, and her little cotton skirt was very crumpled. She walked slowly, as was her habit, and she did not so much as glance towards my window. Then she disappeared among the huts.

Some time later Glahn came down, his rifle under his arm and all ready to go out hunting. He looked morose and said nothing. But he was well turned out and had taken special care about his appearance. Dressed up like a bridegroom, I thought to myself.

I got ready at once and went out with him, and neither of us said a word. The first two birds we shot were horribly mangled because we shot them with rifles; but we roasted them under a tree as best we could and consumed them in silence. So time passed until twelve o'clock.

Glahn shouted to me: 'Are you sure you have loaded? We might run across something unexpectedly. Load, anyhow.'

'I have loaded,' I answered.

Then he disappeared for a moment into the bush. What delight it would give me to shoot him, shoot him down like a dog. There was no hurry, he could be allowed to savour the thought of it for a while, for he knew quite well what was in my mind; that was why he had asked if I had loaded. Even to-day he had not been able to resist indulging his insolent pride; he had got himself all dressed up and put on a new shirt; his manner was arrogant beyond all belief.

About one o'clock he stops before me, pale and angry, and says: 'No, I can't stand it! Do look and see if you have loaded, man, see whether you have anything in your gun.'

'Kindly attend to your own gun,' I answered. But I knew well enough why he was always asking about mine.

And he walked away from me again. My answer had put him so firmly in his place that he seemed chastened, and he hung his head as he walked off.

After a while I shot a pigeon and re-loaded. While I was doing this, Glahn stood half-hidden behind a tree, watching to see if I really was loading; then he starts singing a hymn, a wedding hymn in fact. He sings wedding hymns and puts his best things on, I thought to myself, and in this way he imagines himself to be quite irresistible. Before he had even finished singing, he began walking slowly in front of me, hanging his head and still singing as he walked. Again he kept close before the muzzle of my gun, as if he were thinking: Now it is about to happen, that is why I sing this wedding hymn! But nothing happened yet, and when he came to the end of his singing he had to look back at me.

'I don't suppose we would have shot anything to-day in any case,' he said with a smile, as though to excuse himself and make amends for having sung while out hunting. Yet even at that moment his smile was beautiful; it was as if he were weeping inwardly; and indeed his lips trembled although he pretended to be able to smile at such a solemn moment.

I was no woman, and he saw well enough that he had made no impression on me; he became impatient, turned pale; he circled round me with hasty steps, was to the left of me and then to the right, occasionally stopping and waiting. Suddenly, towards five o'clock, I heard a shot, and a bullet whistled past my left ear. I looked up. Glahn was standing motionless a few paces away staring at me, his smoking rifle rested on his arm. Had he tried to shoot me? I said: 'You missed, you have been shooting badly recently.'

But he had not been shooting badly, he never missed, he had only wanted to provoke me.

'Then in the devil's name take your revenge!' he shouted back.

'All in good time,' I said, clenching my teeth.

We stand looking at each other, and suddenly Glahn shrugs his shoulders and shouts 'Coward!' at me. Why did he have to call me a coward? I threw my rifle to my shoulder, aimed full in his face and fired.

As a man sows, so shall he reap. . . .

But there is now no need for the Glahn family to seek this man any longer; it irritates me constantly to come across their ludicrous advertisements offering such and such a reward for information about a dead man. Thomas Glahn died in an accident, was shot by accident while hunting in India. The court entered his name and the circumstances of his death in a stitched and bound register, and in that register is written that he is dead, I tell you, yes, and even that he was killed by a stray bullet.

# KNUT HAMSUN

IN 1888, when Knut Hamsun was almost thirty, he was starving " in an attic, only three feet from the moon ", and had achieved nothing. Some years before that he had left his uncle's farm among the northern fjords of Norway to embark on a literary career, but without success. Since then he had worked as a schoolmaster and as a labourer, had travelled to America twice, lectured on French Literature in Minneapolis, conducted a tram in Chicago, and sailed as a deckhand to the Grand Banks of Newfoundland.

" It was during the time I walked about and starved in Christiania, in that strange city which no one leaves without having been marked by it . . ." This was the first sentence of an incomplete novel which Hamsun, himself bearing all the marks of extreme distress, took to a publisher in 1888. The fragment appeared in the autumn as *Hunger*, and established Hamsun almost overnight as one of the leading Scandinavian writers.

During the next few years there followed *Mysteries* and *Pan*. The subjective style of writing of these three books was startlingly new at the time, and in many ways it has remained unique to this day. *Mysteries* is the story of an eccentric charlatan who arrives in a small fishing town, sends himself faked telegrams and then, apparently without motive, is at pains to expose himself; his social outrages and unpredictable behaviour occupy and disturb the placid minds of those about him, and cast doubts on the validity of all their ideas.

In 1898 *Victoria* was published, a love story whose effect is as powerful as the writing is light-handed. The most evanescent moods, and the deepest emotions, take hold of one when one reads this book as they do of the characters in it, and yet no passionate words are used; nothing is stated directly, and yet nothing is obscure, and the narrative flows as easily as one's own thoughts.

Hamsun's other books fall mainly into two groups, those that describe the adventures of vagabonds and wanderers, like his stories about America, or *Muted Strings* and *Under Autumn Stars*, and those of the soil, of the return to the land. There are also many short stories, and Hamsun's mastery in the use of almost imperceptible means gives them a quality that sets them apart.

In 1920 the Nobel Prize for Literature was awarded to Knut Hamsun. Until his death in 1952 he lived on an estate he had bought near Grimstad, in southern Norway, where he wrote and farmed.

M.T.B.